Sunny Holiday

Sunny Holiday

COLEEN MURTAGH PARATORE

SCHOLASTIC INC.
New York Toronto London Auckland
Sydney Mexico City New Delhi Hong Kong

This book was originally published in hardcover
by Scholastic Press in 2009.

ISBN-13: 978-0-545-07588-6
ISBN-10: 0-545-07588-2

12 11 10 9 8 7 6 5 4 3 2 1   9 10 11 12 13 14/0

Printed in the U.S.A.   40
First Scholastic paperback printing, September 2009

The text type was set in Apollo MT.
Book design by Lillie Mear

To all the little lions —

bloom, bloom, bloom

— C.M.P.

Mama may have,
Papa may have,
But God bless the child
that's got his own.
— from "God Bless the Child"
by Billie Holiday

✿   ✿   ✿

Sunny Holiday

Contents

CHAPTER ONE

Dandelions

❀ ❀ ❀

A dandelion is a powerful flower.

"Bloom like a dandelion, baby girl." That's what my daddy says.

A dandelion is a powerful flower. There's a "lion" right in its name.

What's so dandy about a dandelion?

A dandelion's little but it ROARS.

Do dandelions need a fancy-pants garden?

No, dandelions do not. They need dirt, air, and rain.

And no matter how hard things ever get, those sunny little lions grow.

Some people hate dandelions, more than dog-doo even. They own yards the size of parks, and they care very much about grass. They like it plain with nothing on top, like pizza without pepperoni. They water it, feed it, sing it to sleep. They love their grass that much. So don't ever walk on it, do you hear me, if you know what's good for you.

Some people spray poison on their grass to keep the weeds away. Dandelions are sure not weeds, but those silly people don't know. It makes them bug-eyed-bee-buzzing-mad seeing tiny yellow circles on their big green squares. They run for their digging shovels and more poison.

But you can't keep a dandelion down. A few days later, just you wait, another little lion finds a way.

We don't have a park or a yard, either, just one long, dirty-gray cement sidewalk.

But that doesn't stop a dandelion. A dandelion seed is smarty-pants-smart. That seed sails off on a wispy balloon, riding free on a summer breeze, search-search-searching for a home. It knows for sure it will find one.

All it sees is sidewalk, sidewalk, sidewalk.

Does it give up?

No, it does not. That little seed keeps searching until it spots a crack.

"Whoopee! Whoopee! Whoopee!" it shouts, and dives in happy for a landing.

But then that seed realizes it's all alone and sits there shaking, not sure just what to do next.

Does it give up?

No, it does not. It sends down a skin-skinny raggedy root, far below, where no one can see, look-look-looking for dirt it can trust. That may take a very long time.

Does it give up?

No, it does not. It finds safe soil and sinks in deep.

One day, a thin stem rises.

Does it let loud noises scare it? Does it let stinky garbage drag it down? Does it worry some old giant shoe will squash it dead for good?

No, it does not. Do you hear me? That lion points its chin up. Up. Up. Up.

I do agree, dandelions have the ug-ugliest leaves, all jaggedy and rough. They have the ug-ugliest old bud heads. You'd never guess something beautiful is coming.

Then after some sun, air, and plain old rain, one day a flower bursts open. "Hello!"

Dandelions are the happiest color yellow, shining like baby suns.

You can't ignore a dandelion. It makes you pay attention.

"Bloom like a dandelion, Sunny." That's what my daddy says.

You bet I will, Daddy. You bet I will. You can count on me. I'll make it all sun-sunny perfect here. Just wait until you come home. Just wait until you see.

Everything will be so sun-sunny perfect, you won't ever leave again.

CHAPTER TWO

Getting Some Jiggle for January

❀   ❀   ❀

A river is a very long thing.

"Jazzy," I say, "we need to get some jiggle for January."

Jazzy Fine is nine, like me, and she's my best friend. She and her mother, Jo-Jo, live one-floor-up-one-railing-over here at Riverview Towers apartments. I'm on the third floor. Jazzy's on the fourth. I can blow her a bubble. She can toss me a ball. So close we don't need a phone.

Riverview Towers is on the bank by the river. The bus-girls up on Hill Street call us the river rats. Those girls couldn't tell a rat from a rabbit, but I'm not saying anything.

Here's the picture from my window: first, the parking lot (stay away from there), then the stinky blue Dumpsters, then the six droop-sorry-straggly trees the mayor planted last year (Jazzy and I got in the newspaper picture!), then the chain-link fence painted mud brown to match the water I guess, then the litterbug-covered rocks, then the railroad tracks, then the dirty old river you don't even want to stick your toes into.

Momma says they are cleaning up the river, good enough to fish in, maybe even swim. They just didn't get to our part yet. A river is a very long thing.

I think the name "Riverview Towers" is a pants-on-fire double lie. The view isn't anything to advertise, and they shouldn't say "towers," plural. There's just this one ugly cement-gray building, like a sidewalk turned up tall, with no pretty tower on top. "Tower" makes it sound like a Cinderella castle. No princesses living here. Three queens, but no princesses.

There's my cat, Queen Jade. Jazzy's cat, Queen Penny. And Jazzy's grandmother, Sister Queen.

Sister Queen is so funny. She cracks me up. If they ever make a TV show called *America's Funniest Grandmothers*, I'm sending her name in for sure.

"What crazy are you talking about now, Sunny?" Jazzy says, stuffing her face with caramel popcorn. "What do you mean, 'get some jiggle for January'?"

It's Saturday, and we're sitting on Jazzy's couch making decorations for the party tonight. It's Girls' Night, and this time we're going to Hawaii.

We've finished the paper-chain flower necklaces, *leis* they're called, and now we're cutting out brown coconuts for the paper palm trees we taped on the walls.

"Think about it," I say. "Poor January. What a month. Nobody likes it. It's cold and dark and boring. It's the first, but it's the worst."

Jazzy giggles.

"Seriously," I say. "How would you feel being stuck between two of the very best months, Santa Claus in December and Valentine's in February, like a slimy old piece of cheese? Doesn't January deserve a fun holiday, too?"

Jazzy nods respectfully up to the picture on the wall. "But what about Dr. King?" she says. "His birthday is in January. That's an important celebration. We just wrote those essays for the school contest, and we're singing with First Baptist at the —"

"I know," I say sincerely. "I'm not trying to take anything away from Reverend King, no way. He gets all the respect. I'm not talking about a write-a-paper-praying-holiday. I'm talking about a fun-happy-party-holiday. I think we should make one up."

"You can't make a holiday, Sunny!" Jazzy shakes her head. "You've got to be the president or the mayor or somebody important like that to make a holiday."

"I am somebody important. And maybe that mayor's so busy planting droop-sorry trees and smiling for the newspaper that he doesn't have time to think about holidays. I am the perfect person for the job. *Holiday* is my *name*."

Jazzy stops cutting coconuts. "I don't know, Sunny."

"Listen," I say. "There are twelve months in a year, right?"

Jazzy nods. "Right."

"Then there should be twelve good holidays. One day a month every kid can look forward to. No school, no work, no worries — just a fun happy day to enjoy, every single month of the year."

"I'm voting for you, girl!" Jazzy says. "Wait, I'll get a calendar." She jumps up, knocking over the bowl of popcorn. When I kneel to pick up the kernels, I see Queen Penny's copper-colored eyes glowing out at me from under the couch.

"Hi, Penny," I say, sticking out my hand. She licks my fingers. I scratch her head.

Jazzy and I got our cats together at the rescue shelter for Christmas. Our mommas surprised us! Took us on the bus two days before Christmas. Jazzy and I agree, they're our best presents ever.

Our cats look like twins, shiny black fur with white paws, except for their eyes. My cat, Queen

Jade, has green eyes, the prettiest ever, nothing against Queen Penny or copper-colored eyes.

Jazzy comes back with a calendar, "Compliments of Health-First Pharmacy," a yellow tablet, and a pen. She writes *HAPPY HOLIDAYS* on the first line of the tablet and then underneath it, *January*.

"Okay, Sunny," she says. "What about January?"

"January needs some jiggle, Jazzy."

Jazzy giggles at me.

"That's got a nice beat," I say, moving my head and shoulders in rhythm. "January needs some *jiggle*, Jazzy. January needs some *jiggle*, Jazzy. January needs some *jiggle*, Jazzy —"

"Okay, okay," Jazzy says, turning the calendar. "What about February?"

"Valentine's is fine," I say. "All the candy and love cards. Maybe you'll get one from

12

Eli this year. Jazzy and Eli sitting in the tree. K-I-S-"

"Cut it out, Sunny," Jazzy says and pushes my arm, laughing. She marks Valentine's Day next to February on our yellow tablet, then turns the page on the Health-First calendar. "How about March?"

We look at the squares. The print is so tiny I put on my ugly green glasses to read.

"There's St. Patrick's Day," I say, "but that's boring. I think March needs help."

"Okay," Jazzy says, turning the calendar page. "What about April?"

"Easter baskets!" we shout like twins.

Jazzy writes *April: Easter*, and I flip the calendar to May.

"There's Mother's Day," Jazzy says, pointing.

"Yes, but that's not a kid's holiday," I say. "Write down 'stay tuned' for May."

Jazzy laughs. I turn to June. "There's Flag Day," I say. "That's important, but it's not really fun."

Jazzy points to Father's Day. She looks at me. Our eyes talk.

"Anyway," Jazzy says, shrugging, "that's not a kid's day, either."

"Hey, wait," I say, a sparkler idea lighting up in my head. "How come there's a Mother's Day and a Father's Day but no *Kid's Day*? That's not fair."

"You're right, Sunny," Jazzy says. "I never thought about that." She looks at the clock. "We gotta hurry. It's almost seven, and we need to borrow the grass skirts from the dance lady." Jazzy turns the calendar to July. She points to the fourth.

"July's fly," I say, and Jazzy agrees.

Every Fourth of July we have a big barbecue with music and games down on the street. We run through the sprinklers and eat ice cream. At night, we light sparklers and chase fireflies, and then we go up on the roof. We spread blankets and lie on our backs and watch the fireworks shooting up across the river from Springtown. Those fireworks are spectacular to see, but I like sparklers better. I can hold a sparkler in my hand.

"Come on, Sunny," Jazzy says, tapping her pen. "What about August?"

"August needs help," I say. "Lots of it."

August is the longest, hottest, meanest month of all. Two years ago, the mayor drained the Riverton town pool for "repairs." It didn't get fixed that summer or last summer, either. Jazzy's grandmother, Sister Queen, said she'll be "up in

Heaven sending down showers to fill that pool before that lazy mayor gets around to it."

"That's wrong they closed our pool," Jazzy says. "Maybe the mayor has a fancy pool at his place, but we sure don't. He ought to think about us."

I nod my head. "You're right, Jazzy. It's time I had a talk with that man. Remind me to have my secretary set up a meeting. Maybe we'll do lunch."

Jazzy giggles. "Okay, Sunny. Let's finish. What about September?"

"Well, there's Labor Day . . . and then back to school."

Jazzy scrunches her nose. "September definitely needs help." She marks that down.

I turn the page to October.

"*Halloween!*" we scream. Jazzy and I were pirates last time. We wore gold bangle earrings and purple eye patches. Momma gave out Milky-Way bars.

"November's got Turkey Day," Jazzy says, flipping the page. *"Yum, yum, yum.* And December's got Santa Claus."

"Okay," I say, studying our list, counting. "I say it's double sixes. February, April, July, October, November, and December all have fun holidays. It's the other six that need help: January, March, May, June, August, and September."

"That's a lot of months," Jazzy says. "Are we going to make *six* new holidays, Sunny, or just one for January?"

"I don't know yet," I say. "Let's do one month at a time." I count the number of days between Christmas and Valentine's Day. About fifty days. A good place for a new January holiday might be in the middle, right around January twentieth. I circle it.

"That's it," I announce.

"What's it?" Jazzy asks.

"The new holiday."

"Yay!" Jazzy says. "What's it going to be? What are we going to call it?"

"I don't know. That's all the sparklers I've got for now. My brain's fried eggs."

Jazzy stares at January on the calendar. "Today is January second," she says. "Back to school Monday. We don't have much time to make a holiday by the twentieth."

"Don't worry, January," I say, patting the page. "We'll jiggle you up somehow."

"*Jiggle?*" Jazzy says, excited. "I know! How about something with *Jell-O!*"

Jazzy loves Jell-O jigglers. Lime is her favorite. Strawberry's mine. "Good idea," I say. "Write that down and let's keep our thinking nets open."

That's what our teacher, Miss Lullaby, says. "Let's keep our thinking nets open." Jell-O's fun, but it's been done. Nothing new about Jell-O jigglers. I don't say that to Jazzy, though. You can squish a person's good imagination if you say something bad too quickly. Miss Lullaby says, "New ideas are fragile. You've got to treat them gentle as a butterfly."

"Come on, Sunny," Jazzy says. "We've got to get the grass skirts now. That crazy lady might change her mind, and then we won't be able to hula."

CHAPTER THREE

Pig and Pineapple Pizza

❀   ❀   ❀

*Every night I count
ten reasons to be grateful.*

Miss Fontenot down in 2-G used to be a famous dancer — Jazzy and I saw the posters in her apartment — but her mind went fruit-loops, and now she does crazy things like ballet dancing in the snow wearing a fuzzy tutu, but no coat. Miss Fontenot used to run a dance school, too. She lets us borrow costumes. We invite her to our parties, but she always says no. I guess she prefers to dance alone.

When Jazzy and I get back with our arms full of the tickly grass skirts, my mother, Sherry, and Jazzy's mother, Jo-Jo, are laughing loud in the kitchen. They are best friends, too. With my daddy gone for a while and Jazzy's daddy probably gone forever, Sherry and Jo-Jo count on each other like family.

The doorbell rings and, whoopee, the party starts. Saturday night is Girls' Night. Momma and Jo-Jo started it as a moms-and-daughters dance party, just the four of us, but word spread and it grew and grew, and now lots of other ladies and girls from the building come. Everybody takes turns hosting. There's a different theme each time, and we all dress up fancy or fun. There's yummy food, good music, and only one rule: Everybody dances. Dance, dance, dance! "Dance your pants off," Sister Queen says. Jazzy and I just love that rule.

Jo-Jo greets each guest at the door with a hug. "Aloha, and welcome to Hawaii!"

Mrs. Gordon and Mrs. Hartman from downstairs are first to arrive. Jo-Jo puts the flower leis Jazzy and I made around their necks.

We pass out the grass skirts. Mirrors from the beauty shop where Jo-Jo works are lined up along the wall like a dance studio. The lights Jazzy and I strung over the palm trees have all turned into stars.

"Hawaii is *beautiful*," my momma says, looking around, smiling.

The smell of pizza floats through the air. We have a different kind each time. The toppings depend on the party theme. I'm curious what they eat in Hawaii, but I sure hope they like pepperoni.

Jo-Jo turns on the music. "Let's dance!" She rolls up the bottom of her shiny gold shirt and ties it in a knot, letting her belly hang out. We all copy her. Young bellies, old bellies, big bellies, skinny bellies, black bellies, vanilla bellies, all sorts of bellies in a row. My skinny belly is milk-chocolate colored. Jazzy's skinny belly is butterscotch.

"Socks and shoes off," Jo-Jo says. "Barefoot is best. Now sink your soles in that soft, warm sand. *Hmmm, hmmm.* Right sole down, left sole up, left sole down, right sole up, that's the rhythm. Now shake those hips, girlfriends. That's it. Shake-shake-a-bake those hips."

Jazzy and I shake and giggle and sing, "Hoo-*la*! Hoo-*la*, hoo-*laaaaaa*!"

"Keep shake-a-baking," Jo-Jo says, moving her hips side to side. "Now sway those palm tree arms to the left, now sway them to the right. Oh, that sun feels good, doesn't it, girls? And just look at that big blue ocean, *hmmm, hmmm.* Almost as pretty as us."

Jazzy and I lock eyes and giggle even more.

"Pump it up, Sherry," Jo-Jo says, and my mother turns up the volume. Then we're all dancing, everybody. Mommas and grandmommas, teenagers, too. Big girls, little girls, even some babies, all dancing together, grass skirts swishing, palm trees sway-swaying, our faces all sweat-shining happy.

"Hu-*la!* Hu-*la*, hoooo-*laaaaa* . . ." Jazzy and I sing loud like we're on a TV show. We climb up on the table-stage to dance, singing and shaking and giggling so much my hula-belly is starting to hurt. But it's a happy hurt.

"Sunny," Momma calls up to me, dancing. "Don't you just love Hawaii?"

"Yes!" I say. "Let's stay all week." I'm happy to see Momma happy. She works so hard for us cleaning rooms at the Crowne Plaza hotel all day, then studying for college at night.

"Jo-Jo," someone shouts from the kitchen. "The oven's buzzing."

"Okay, okay," Jo-Jo says. "Pizza time!" She turns down the music. "Jazzy, you and Sunny serve the punch, please. Jazzy made the recipe herself, everybody."

We gather around the table. The punch bowl is filled with sparkling soda. "There are four kinds of sherbet — raspberry, orange, lemon, and lime — all mixed together," Jazzy says proudly. There's a little umbrella-on-a-toothpick in each of our cups. I pick the dandelion-yellow umbrella. Yellow is my favorite color.

"We got a whole pack of twenty umbrellas at Daisy's," Jazzy whispers to me. Daisy's Lucky Buck is the dollar store we love to shop at. Jazzy is whispering because our mommas taught us that a hostess should be gracious and not go talking about how much all of the party stuff cost.

I swish my umbrella and take a sip, my pinkie finger sticking out all fancy. "*Mmmm*, my compliments to the hostess. Would you care to share the recipe, madam?"

Jazzy giggles and then composes herself. She raises her chin and sticks her pinkie out, too. "Why certainly, *dahling*. I'll ask my butler to jot it down for you."

My stomach lion-growls for pizza. All that dancing made me hungry.

"What kind are we having?" I ask Sister Queen.

"Pig and pineapple," Sister Queen says, pushing up her nose with her finger, *snort, snort.*

"*Pig?*" I say. "That's nasty. I'm not eating some old *oinky-oink* pig! Are you, Jazzy?"

Sister Queen is smiling, her pretty white teeth shining bright.

"Not me." Jazzy shakes her head, disgusted. "Momma didn't say anything about a pig. That's dog-turd nasty."

"It's worse than that," I say. "*Pig pizza?* That's dog-turd-topping-on-your-ice-cream nasty."

"It's nastier than that," Jazzy says. "It's pick-a-booger-paste-it-on-your-math-book nasty."

"Oh, no!" Sister Queen says, eyes bugging out, pointing toward the kitchen like she's scared. "Oh, no! That pig didn't get cooked enough, Jo-Jo. It's alive! Oh, no! Here it comes! *Oink . . . oink . . .*"

Jazzy and I scream.

"Run, babies, quick! He's coming," Sister Queen shouts. "And, oh, it's one of those giant sharp-tooth —"

"*Sister Queen*," my momma says, laughing. "Please stop teasing those girls."

Everybody's laughing, Sister Queen most of all. She wipes her eyes and blows her nose on one of the fancy pink party napkins with palm trees on them that also came from Daisy's Lucky Buck.

"I'm sorry," Sister Queen says. "Come here, babies." She opens her arms wide to hug me on the left, Jazzy on the right. We fit perfect. Sister kisses my head. She smells like coconuts. Her black hair is streaked with silver, like a veil for a royal lady.

Oh, and by the way. "Pig" is ham. *Hallelujah!* Jo-Jo says they do pig roasts at luau parties in Hawaii. Roasting a pig sounds nasty to me, but the ham and pineapple pizza tastes delicious, almost as good as pepperoni.

"I do love Hawaii," I tell Momma.

"Me, too," she says. "I'm glad we made the trip. Perfect weather, delicious food, good friends." Momma finishes her sherbet drink and sticks her orange umbrella on her sweater like a flower corsage on Easter Sunday.

"Where are we traveling to next, Momma?" I say. "It's our turn to host."

"I'm not sure," Momma says. "Remind me to call my travel agent in the morning and get that guy working on it." She winks at me and we laugh.

After we say good-bye, Momma and I take the fire-escape stairs up to the roof. In the summer, we call it the beach. The stairway smells like pee, and it's a good thing we put our shoes back on, because you don't want to step on broken glass. When we reach the top, Momma pushes open the door.

The beach is cold and dark and windy. I look up at the sky. It's our Saturday night tradition.

"Same moon shining on Daddy," I say.

"That's right, baby. Pick a star."

When I finish wishing, I open my eyes. Momma turns away quickly, wiping her face. I don't let her know that I see. She tries to be brave for me.

"Time for bed, Sunny," Momma says. "We've got a long trip tomorrow."

Down in our apartment, I brush my teeth singing the "Happy Birthday" song one-two-three-four times in a row. That's the trick Miss Judy at the dentist's office taught me. She said you have to brush your teeth just that long to get them really clean.

It's cold in my bedroom. I put on my fuzzy banana slipper-socks and snuggle under the soft, warm quilt Grand-Gran sent me for Christmas. She used all different kinds of yellow patches. *A sunny quilt for my Sunny girl*, she wrote on the card. I wish Grand-Gran didn't live so far away. North Carolina. We only get to see each other at the summer reunion. Good thing Jazzy shares Sister Queen with me.

I read a chapter of my book and close it back on my nightstand. Before I shut off the light, I lift my hands up near my face, palms toward me, and I look at my fingers. Every night I count ten reasons to be grateful. Momma taught me to pray like that. On especially good days, toes can be added.

I start with my left thumb and count off: "Thank you, God, for Momma, Daddy, Jazzy, Hawaii, and hula-hula-dancing." Then I move to my right-hand pinkie. "And pig-and-pineapple pizza, umbrella drinks, Sister Queen, wishing stars, and Visiting Day tomorrow."

Then I cross my palms over my heart. "Good night."

CHAPTER FOUR

Visiting Day

❁　　❁　　❁

We'll have breakfast on the ship.

When I wake up, *good morning*, it's snowing. I smell something delicious baking. *Mmmmm*. I close my eyes, and then I remember. Visiting Day! I jump out of bed and run to the kitchen.

Momma's listening to FLY 92 Chief Meteorologist Manny Marino. "Winter storm warning . . . snow turning to sleet and freezing rain . . .

motorists strongly cautioned against driving unless necessary —"

Visiting Day is sure necessary. It's the first Sunday of the month.

The one day I get to see my daddy.

I haven't seen him since before Halloween.

In November, there was an "internal lockdown problem" and no visitors were allowed. Momma had to mail Daddy the cornucopia Thanksgiving place mat I made for him at school. I don't know if he got it in time for his turkey dinner. I don't even know if he had turkey. He forgot to say in his letter.

Then, in December, Momma and I were all set to go, coats on and everything, when the phone rang and Momma got called in to work. Her boss, Mr. Feeney, such a mean-meanie, didn't care one "stinking bit" about Visiting Day or anybody's "personal problems." The hotel was booked solid, three girls were out sick, and those suites at the Crowne Plaza weren't going to clean themselves, now were they? No, sir.

I saw one of those suite rooms once. It was bigger than our whole apartment.

Momma shuts off the radio. "Oh, good, Sunny. You're up. Let's leave before the weather gets bad. I packed muffins and cocoa. We'll have breakfast on the ship."

"Banana muffins?"

"Yep."

"Hoorah!"

I hurry to my room to get dressed. My ugly green glasses scare me in the mirror. Daddy hasn't seen them yet. I hope he still thinks I'm pretty.

The glasses are that no-smile nurse's fault. At my physical in August, I was waiting and waiting in that hot and smelly little room, and finally the no-smile nurse came in and said, "*Ugh, what a day*. Okay, cover your right eye and read the letters in the third line down." She didn't even say my name. How did she even know it was me?

"E . . . O . . . J . . . . M . . . . . S . . . . . ."
I only got three right.

After, I was mad, because I could have memorized all those letters, every row, I was waiting so long for that lady.

I squirt oil onto my palms and smooth my hair. Jo-Jo tied on yellow marble beads when she did my braids for Christmas Eve. I might look nice if it wasn't for these Jolly Green Giant glasses. That's what the bus-girls called them. They thought that was hysterical.

Someday I'll get contact lenses and abracadabra, *whoosh*, I'll be Cinderella.

I put on my favorite yellow sweater and my new jeans with the yellow flower pockets. Momma got the pants at the Salvation Army and then stitched on the flowers to make them original. Momma works magic making old clothes new. She buys fancy buttons and sequins on sale at Crafty Lady and sews in designer labels, "Sherry Chic."

I stuff Daddy's presents in a shopping bag. Thirty envelopes all marked *Daddy*. One happy picture he can look forward to opening every day until I see him again. My pictures aren't as good as Daddy's, no way. He's the artist in the family. But I did my best. And because January is the darkest, dreariest month of all, I put smiling yellow suns in all the skies and sunny dandelions everywhere.

Some people might not know this, but dandelions are so special you can't even buy them at a flower store. You have to wait until they grow naturally.

Daddy will love my present. He would also

love a juicy steak or Momma's fudge brownies, but food gifts are sure not allowed in prison.

We take the elevator to the first floor. Nice Mrs. Gordon in 1-C lets us borrow her "ship" on Visiting Day. It's an old black Cadillac. Mrs. Gordon doesn't use it very much because she can't see over the wheel without sitting on a hill of pillows. The ship was her husband's. He died. Mrs. Gordon won't take money for gas. Good thing because we don't have any extra money. Mrs. Gordon says to Momma, "We're friends, Sherry, that's all. Now please don't insult me. I have more fun dancing at your parties than I've had in fifty years."

Momma found a good way to thank Mrs. Gordon, though. Each time we borrow the ship, Momma makes a chicken stew or beef chili or something delicious and divides it into one-person-size freezer bags, so when Mrs. Gordon wants a nice home-cooked meal, she can just "pop one in the microwave." My momma is so smart like that.

In the parking lot, Momma turns on the car and we sweep snow off the windows with our broom. I sit up front on Mrs. Gordon's pillows. We buckle up.

"Ready to sail?" Momma says.

"Yes, captain, ma'am."

"We'll be first in line," Momma says. Visiting Day is one to four.

Mount Burden Correctional Facility is three hours from Riverton. Usually there are lots of cars and trailer trucks on the highway. I like to see how many different state license plates I can spot. Once I saw one from California! Today, it's a ghost road.

Momma drives slow, hands tight on the wheel, staring straight ahead. The snow is falling beautifully. The wiper blades are *swish-swish-swishing* away. It's toasty snug in here. I unwrap a warm banana muffin for Momma and put it on a napkin on her lap. I sip cocoa from my thermos. *Mmmm.*

"Excuse me, Miss DJ," Momma says. "Are you taking requests yet?"

"Yes, ma'am." I turn on the radio and find a good song. Momma and I sing it loud together. My momma has the best voice in the whole First Baptist Choir — and that's saying something. People are always telling Momma she should send out tapes to recording studios. She could be famous, for sure. Momma gets bright-eyed bashful and says thank you, but waves them away with their "crazy talk." Singing at First Baptist is fine by her.

I know Momma could be famous. And I wouldn't ever have to wait in line for her

autograph because I'm her very own daughter.
Last year, Grand-Gran sent me a shiny gold autograph book for my birthday. So far it's empty.
Famous people don't come to Riverton. They do
come to Springtown, though. They perform at The
Palace or the Civic Center, and they stay at the
hotel where Momma works. I would sure like to
meet some stars and get their autographs, but
Momma's boss, Mr. Feeney, such a meanie, gave
strict orders: "Don't ever ask guests for autographs.
Once, and you're fired. Do you hear me?" Yes, sir.

Our ship sails slowly out of the city, past tall
buildings, then shorter buildings until it's all trees
and hills painted with snow. January doesn't
seem that bad out here.

I start thinking about Kid's Day. What's it
going to be like? On Mother's Day, I always give
Momma a card and serve her breakfast in bed.
On Father's Day, I give Daddy a card and serve

him breakfast in bed. Well, that might work just fine for them — and they always seem so appreciative — but Kid's Day is going to have to be way better than breakfast in bed, even if it's a triple-tall stack of chocolate-chip pancakes with bacon and sausage on the side.

I smile at the cows walking single file into an old red barn. There's a gray horse and a pony and then three big, dark, funny-looking birds. "Are they *turkeys*?" I ask Momma.

She looks quick. "Yep."

I laugh and shake my head. "It's a zoo out here."

I eat another one of Momma's famous banana muffins with cinnamon sugar on top, and I read her a chapter of my book for school. I always read every day, no matter what.

After that, I'm a little sleepy. I rest my head

back and look out the window, all that white, snowy world *whoosh-whooshing* by. A deer darts out of the forest up ahead, then another. They stand there staring at the road. Then a bigger deer with horns runs out and all three start galloping. They're going to run right in front of us! "Momma!" I say. "Watch out!"

Momma brakes hard and the ship swirls back. Momma *tap-tap-taps* the brakes, and we twirl like that carnival ride that came to the Kmart parking lot, round and round and round. Other cars honk their horns, tires screech, and we *sliiiiide* off the road. . . . *Thump!* I jolt forward-back.

"Are you okay, baby?" Momma shouts, taking my face in her hands.

"Yes." My body's shaking like hula hips. "Are you?"

"Yep." Momma bites her lip.

"Good thing we buckled up," I say. Momma hugs me tight.

We get out and check the ship. Everything looks okay, but we have a big problem. The car is in a ditch, and the tires are stuck in the snow. We don't have a phone to call anyone. Momma wraps her pink wool scarf around the antenna. "Let's wait in the ship," she says.

We wait a very long time. A huge snowplow barrels by dumping more snow our way. Momma smiles and says, "Let's say a little prayer." We close our eyes.

A lady in a big silver car-truck stops. We get out to talk to her.

"I'll call for help," the lady says, her words making smoke signals in the winter air. Then up goes her window and, good-bye, she's gone.

Help takes a very long time. The snow changes to ice chips that sting my face and crackle as they hit the ground. We wait in the ship again. I'm cold. Momma checks her watch and sighs. She winks at me and says, "Don't worry."

Finally, a huge white tow truck comes, with a sparkly American flag on the side. "Hoorah!" I say. "God is good," Momma says. We hurry back out of the ship.

The driver is bundled up like an Eskimo. He smiles at me and says, "What are you, an icicle? Hop up in the truck and get warm."

It smells like cigarettes in here, *pee-you*. The man and Momma are talking.

"Well, who's going to pay for this?" the man shouts. He opens the truck door, not smiling anymore. "Come on down out of there," he says to me.

My stomach's flip-flopping scared.

A police car comes, red light swirling. Momma and the officer and the truck driver talk. Momma says, "No, I'm sorry. I don't have a roadside-assistance policy."

The officer tells the driver something. The driver shakes his head and huffs. He goes up into his truck and comes back with a clipboard. Lots of papers are filled out and signed. The officer tells me and Momma to get into the police car. "I'll take you to the station to warm up," he says.

The mad-Eskimo driver attaches chains to Mrs. Gordon's car and hauls it up on the back of his truck. "The tire's busted," he says. "It's going to take a while to fix."

Oh, no. Not too long, please. I push Momma's glove back and check her watch.

It takes a long time to get to the police station. The officer asks Momma where she got the car from. He calls Mrs. Gordon, but she's not home. The officer gets another call and tells us to wait; he'll be right back. Momma and I wait and wait and wait. I watch the time go by on the big black clock, my stomach clenching into a fist.

Finally, the officer gets through to Mrs. Gordon. She was visiting Mrs. Hartman in 1-H for their weekly Sunday Scrabble match. She "verified" that we borrowed her car. I'm so fuming mad I could spit. Did that man think my momma was lying? My momma never lies. I could have told him that a long time ago and saved him the trouble.

The officer offers me a lollipop for "being so good."

"No, thank you," I say, not even looking at his eyes.

By the time he finally drives us to the repair place to get Mrs. Gordon's car back, it is 4:15 P.M. and Visiting Day is sure over.

The ride home feels two hundred hours long, my forehead pressed against the cold glass, lights whizzing by in the dark.

"I'll mail Daddy your present first thing in the morning," Momma says.

I stare out at the night.

"Come on," Momma says, all cheerful. "Let's splurge!"

She pulls over at a rest area, and we wait in line for hamburgers. When Momma goes to get more napkins, I slide my fries into the garbage. I have lost my appetite.

Queen Jade runs to greet me when we get home. "Hey, Jadie." I pick her up and cuddle her soft to my face. "I missed you, girl." When I put her down, she rubs against my leg, then runs to the kitchen. I brush her, feed her, and scoop the litter box.

In bed, I reach for my teddy bear, Valentine,

and hug him extra-extra-hard tight. Daddy gave him to me last Valentine's Day, just before he left for that "quick job" and made that "very big mistake."

Daddy is always going away and coming back soon. He loves me and Momma, but he hates Riverton. He says it's dead, nothing good for him here. He says if a man stays here too long, he gets stuck in the sidewalk forever. Not me, though, no way. Daddy says I'm going to bloom like a dandelion.

My daddy is an artist. He's going to be famous someday. You wait and see. There's a big, brown leather zip portfolio of his sketches under his bed. I sneak it out to look sometimes. Daddy draws faces so real it's almost like they are pictures from a camera. You can feel what the people are feeling. Happy, sad, joyful, scared. The eyes are the best. You can see the person's whole story in them.

Daddy tells Momma he just needs "one big break." I know my daddy's good enough and I believe his big break is coming. I just think when he sets off to find it, he ought to take his portfolio with him. How else is anybody going to see his talent? Nobody's going to see it hiding under the bed.

Daddy wants to buy a big house for me and Momma with a yard and a garden and swings, but it's hard to make good money without a college degree. Daddy had a summer job with a lawn-mowing company and a winter job washing dishes at the hospital, but he wasn't proud of that work. He kept getting sadder. Then one Sunday, Daddy's old friend Bluesky showed up after church. Bluesky was dressed sly and had a big, shiny car everybody was crowding around to touch. Bluesky said he had an offer for Daddy, a real fine, big-paying job. I heard Momma and Daddy arguing that night and Momma crying. When Daddy kissed me good-bye the next morning, he said, "I'll be back real soon, baby. I promise. And then everything will be better — just you wait and see."

I squeeze Valentine so extra-hard tight fluffy stuffing pops out of the top of his head. I stuff the fluff back in. "I love you, Valentine. You're a good bear."

I turn on the light by my bed and read. The boy in the book is having his palm read at a carnival. I look at the palm of my left hand up close in the light. There are three lines. One line is stretched straight across the middle. The other two lines are curved down, with little roots on the ends. The two curved lines are attached at the top. The straight line comes close but doesn't quite touch the other two.

I bring both palms up close to my face. There

wasn't anything, not one single thing, good about today. I shut off my light. I think of some things. I turn it back on and start counting with my left thumb: "Thank you, God, for Momma, Daddy, Mrs. Gordon's ship, radio songs, banana muffins, my shiny gold autograph book, the zoo, Queen Jadie, Valentine, and Daddy's portfolio."

I cross my hands over my heart. "Good night."

CHAPTER FIVE

"Free All Year"

❀ ❀ ❀

*We are writing that book
on our living room wall.*

Momma makes oatmeal for breakfast in the morning. She stirs in raisins and brown sugar and pours warm milk on top. "I've got to catch the 6:48," she says, rushing around our closet-sized kitchen. She zips her lunch pack and twists the top on her thermos. I eat a sweet spoonful of oatmeal.

Momma takes the bus to work every day with

lots of people from our building. They work at the stores and hotels and hospitals and restaurants across the river in Springtown.

Momma puts on her hat, coat, and gloves. "Be sure to dress warm," she says.

I hope Momma gets a seat on the bench inside the plastic graffiti house so she won't freeze waiting for the bus. "Okay, Momma. I will."

"I need to get in early," Momma says. "I want to ask Mr. Feeney for extra hours. And I know you don't like it, Sunny, but please go to Mrs. Sherman's place after school. I'll pick you up by six. I promise." Usually I go to Jazzy's after school, but today Sister Queen is taking Jazzy to the dentist.

Momma kisses my forehead. "Your lunch is in the fridge. I love you, baby. Have a good day."

"Love you, too, Momma."

I lock the door and stand on the stool to pull the chain. Good thing for Queen Jade. I pick her up and scratch her, and she purrs to say she's happy. I pour some milk on a plate, and she laps it up while I finish breakfast.

Momma needs extra hours to pay that mad-Eskimo tow-truck man. "Roadside assistance" is a very expensive thing. I heard Momma telling Jo-Jo last night, "It's more than I make all week."

Too bad those deer didn't wait for a green light or something before they galloped across the road in front of us. That would have been a good thing.

Momma and I are experts on good things. We're writing a book on that topic. We are writing that book on our living room wall, but it sure is not graffiti. We're using markers that wash right off, and someday soon, when our book gets published and we make a million dollars and move to our big yellow house with the porch up on Hill Street where the bus-girls live, we'll paint the wall fresh before we leave.

Momma and I hope Oprah Winfrey will like our book and invite us to be on her show. Then we'll be *famous*. Then *we* can sign my autograph book and maybe Oprah will, too! I would love to meet Oprah. *Hope-rah*. That's what she gives people. Hope.

Momma and Jo-Jo love Oprah like a sister, even though they only talk to her through the TV. Jo-Jo tapes the shows all week because she and Momma are working when it's on. They do an "Oprah Marathon" on Sunday after church and our brunchfest. That's the half breakfast–half lunch we have on Sundays when it's not Visiting Day.

Jazzy and I roll our eyes and giggle watching Jo-Jo and Momma talk to Oprah. They act like she can really see and hear them through the screen.

"That's right, Oprah," Momma says, hands up in the air like she's testifying.

"*Hmmm, hmmmm*, girl. You tell it," Jo-Jo says, nodding her head like a hammer up and down. "That's right, Ms. O. That's the truth."

Momma says she might invite Oprah to Girls' Night sometime.

Jo-Jo says, "You never know, Sherry. She just might come."

Then those bus-girls will have something *real* to talk about!

I wash the dishes and set them on the ledge to dry. There's the picture of me and Jazzy and the mayor on the refrigerator. Jazzy and I were so happy because we thought we were going to get a real park with swings and slides and trees to climb.

But all we got were six droop-sorry sticks, way too wimpy-woozy to climb.

In the living room, I stop to admire our beautiful wall book. Just wait until Daddy sees! Momma and I started our book on New Year's Eve. We had finished our fancy food — mini hot dogs, potato skins, pizza poppers, and fizzy ginger ale with extra cherries — and while we were waiting for the rock-and-roll ball to drop, we started our "wish list poster." We make one every New Year's Eve. It's a Holiday family tradition.

First we wished Daddy was here. He's not up for parole until June, though. Momma says parole is looking good because Daddy has had very good behavior. Daddy is very sorry for his big mistake and says it won't ever happen again.

I blame Daddy's flashy-car-friend, Bluesky. It was all his idea. Daddy just got crazy excited and didn't count-to-ten-and-think-again before he ran off to join him. Daddy is always trying to find a fast way to get us out of Riverton. Momma says there's no shortcut. That's why she's working hard and taking college classes, too. Momma can only take one class at a time, but one day she'll get that degree. I'll be so proud of her.

The next wish we wrote on our poster was that Grand-Gran and Jazzy and Jo-Jo and all of our relatives and friends and everyone we know would stay safe and healthy.

Then we started listing other stuff. Momma had to write fast to get all my wishes down. Disneyland, a cell phone, a laptop computer. And one of those fancy dolls that have their own restaurant in New York City. A bus-girl said that when you take your doll there, she gets her own chair and food, too! And I kept on wishing . . . clothes from the mall and bunk beds for when Jazzy sleeps over and a TV for my room . . .

Momma kept writing, but soon after, her face stopped smiling.

And me, well, I was getting sadder and sadder just thinking about how we could never afford to buy this or that thing, and finally Momma put the pen down and stared at me, hard.

"Sunny Holiday, listen. Money can't buy a happy heart. You and I have happy hearts. We aren't millionaires, but we're *rich*. Don't believe anything different."

That sounded nice, but I kept looking at my wish list.

"I have an idea," Momma said, all excited. "Come on." She stood up, took my hand, and pulled me up, too. "Let's write everything we love that's *free* . . . on the wall."

"On the wall?" My eyes were bee-bugging out. *"Are you sure?"*

"Very sure," Momma said, smiling. My momma's so pretty when she smiles.

Momma picked up a purple marker. Purple is her favorite color.

I laughed and picked up a yellow. That's how it all started.

The wall was Momma's idea. Making it a book was mine.

It's called *Free All Year.*

Now every time Momma and I think of something that makes us happy that is *free* — you don't have to pay even a penny for it, or clip a coupon for it, or give it back or anything — we write it on the wall.

This is the first line of our book:

The things we love best are free all year.

Momma and I decided that since there are 365

days in a year, we should think of 365 things, one for each day. Happy free things like rainbows.

Love was Momma's first wall-word.

Family was mine.

Then Momma wrote *Singing*. And I wrote *Dancing*.

Momma wrote *Friends*. I wrote *Dandelions*. We looked at that word and giggled. Momma hugged me tight, and right then the ball dropped. *Happy New Year!* We rock-and-rolled with everyone on TV. I wondered if Daddy was watching, too.

Our book is off to a very good start. We have twenty-three free things so far. I figure we should be finished by Valentine's Day, published into a book by the Fourth of July, on the *Oprah* show by Halloween, and famous by Thanksgiving.

CHAPTER SIX

Mrs. Lullaby's Silver Suitcase

❀   ❀   ❀

She looks us right in the eyes like we're real.

Jazzy and I walk sister-twin-together six blocks down the street to New Hope Charter School. The mayor threw a party when New Hope opened. Jazzy and I wiggled our way right up next to the mayor and got in the picture, but now our principal, Mr. Otis, says we're on the "danger list," and we might have to close.

According to those big tests they make us take every year, New Hope Charter School is at the bottom of the barrel. Now we have extra homework every night and practice tests on Friday so New Hope will do better next time. Until then, we're "on probation" and that's a very bad thing.

I'm confused, though, because I thought "probation" was a good thing. It means you're out of jail. And as long as you don't make any more mistakes, you get to be free again.

At the corner, Jazzy and I wait for the light. A man comes out of Mrs. Milo's store and stands there scratching off a lottery ticket. He tosses it on the ground, nasty old litterbug, and walks off.

"Sister Queen gave us each a dollar for the new year," Jazzy says.

"Great!" I say. Now we can stop at Mrs. Milo's for a treat after school.

The light changes, and Jazzy and I walk. The street isn't plowed, but we don't care. We stomp through the dirty, slushy snow like Eskimos in our matching red boots. Every year the Levy twins up in 5-H pass down their last year's boots to us. Jazzy and I are twins, too. Sister-twins. Different mommas, different birthdays, sister-twins just the same.

We pass the pink door of Crowns of Glory, the beauty shop where Jazzy's mother, Jo-Jo, works, then Chico's Bar-B-Q, *mmm-yumm*, then Daisy's Lucky Buck, our favorite store. We stop and look in the window. Still all the Christmas stuff. When we pass Mid-Nite's Bar and Grill, we lock arms, faces straight ahead, walking faster. Everyone knows to stay away from that place, if you know what's good for you. Our friend Birdy's brother got shot there.

I'm still thinking about Visiting Day and how I

didn't get to see Daddy, but I don't say anything to Jazzy. At least I know where my daddy is. Jazzy's father left when we were in kindergarten. I don't even remember what he looks like. Jazzy used to get a thought-that-counts present from him on Christmas and on her birthday. Now just Christmas. I think he forgot when her birthday is.

Jazzy's birthday is May twenty-first.

"Sunny, how's the new holiday coming?" Jazzy asks.

"Not too good yet," I say. "All I know is it's going to be better than breakfast in bed."

"Well, what's it going to be like?" Jazzy persists. "Are we going to get presents like Christmas or dress up like Halloween or get baskets like on Easter?"

No sparklers are sparking in my head as Jazzy talks. But that's okay because now we're at school, and sparklers aren't allowed here anyway.

Mr. Otis, our never-smile principal — maybe he's related to that no-smile nurse who made me get these glasses — is standing on the top step at the entrance to school. "Move along, move along," he says, waving his hand back and forth, looking out over our heads like he's herding sheep.

That man is cold. He never looks at me.

"Good morning, Mr. Otis," I shout up to him, respectful, but loud, trying to make him look.

He doesn't. He just *tap-tap-taps* his pointer finger on his lips. I sure bet he's thinking about that "danger list." Someday, after we get out of probation, I'm going to make that man see me.

And then, we're inside.

Shhhhhhhhhhhhhhhhhhh.

Once you step foot in New Hope Charter School, you better follow the rules, for sure. No talking, touching, eating, drinking, whispering, whistling, laughing, loafing, giggling, wiggling, running, humming, hitting, skipping, jumping, bumping, burping, *nothing*. No water fountain, no bathroom, no stopping to read the honor roll names or admire the fifth graders' new under-the-sea paintings in the hallway display case, no matter how sparkly pretty they are. So what are they there for? Around here, it's eyes straight ahead, single file, march to your classroom, *now*.

Jazzy and I are in the same fourth-grade class, good thing. We have Mrs. Lucretia Lullaby, lucky us. She's the oldest and nicest teacher in the school, in the world maybe. I love her very much. All the kids do. She looks us right in the eyes like we're real.

Jazzy and I have been in the same class since kindergarten. Then, this year, somebody made a big "paperwork mistake." I got Mrs. Lullaby and Jazzy got Mr. Rooney. That wasn't going to work. Jazzy and I cried and cried the whole first week of school, and finally they fixed that paperwork mistake.

The sign on our classroom door says: *Mrs. Lullaby's Smarties.*

When I first read that sign in September, I got worried. Nobody ever called me a "smarty" before. But then I met Mrs. Lullaby and every-thing was fine. Whenever our class works extra hard learning something, Mrs. Lullaby gives us each a little roll of Smarties candy. "My smarties deserve Smarties!" she says.

I hang my yellow backpack and lunch bag in my locker and take my seat in the second row, second seat, right across from Jazzy. Good thing there's no school rule against looking at your best friend and talking with your eyes.

We all fold our hands on our desks and wait.

"Good morning, good people of the world!" Mrs. Lullaby says, sweeping into the room like a rainbow on foot, smiling like "thank goodness vacation is over."

We stand like rows of paper dolls. "Good morning, Mrs. Lullaby!"

"Thank you," she says. "What a lovely greeting. Please be seated, class."

Mrs. Lullaby sets her silver suitcase on her desk. The suitcase is covered with stickers from amusement parks. Mrs. Lullaby loves to ride roller coasters, especially Wildcats. Her dream is to ride one in every state. She has forty-three to go.

I look out the window. It's snowing. I sit up straight in my chair. Mr. Otis does his never-smile announcements on the intercom. We stand for the Pledge of Allegiance, then sit back down again.

"Now then," Mrs. Lullaby says in a quiet voice, soft and soothing like her name. I lean forward to hear. Everyone else does, too. We don't want to miss a word.

"Welcome back, smarties. It's January. A brand-new beautiful year stretching out fresh before us. I'm so excited to begin learning together again!"

Mrs. Lullaby always says "learning together." I think that's funny because Mrs. Lullaby has to be at least fifty. She must know everything by now.

"Before we begin," Mrs. Lullaby says, "I have a feeling you may have carried three bags to school with you today, just like the Billy Goats Gruff."

Jazzy and I look at each other and eye-giggle like always.

"Let me inquire, good people," Mrs. Lullaby says. "Have you put your book bags away?"

"Yes, Mrs. Lullaby."

"Good, that's one," Mrs. Lullaby says. "And have you put your lunch bags away?"

"Yes, Mrs. Lullaby."

"Good, that's two." Mrs. Lullaby opens her silver suitcase and shows us what's inside.

It's empty like always.

"Now," she says. "Let's take care of that third bag you hauled into school on your little backs today. Any worries you carried with you that make it hard to learn. . . ." As Mrs. Lullaby talks, she walks down the first aisle, stopping at each desk so kids can drop their worries inside the suitcase.

When she gets to me, I put my hands up to my head and make believe I'm pull-pull-pulling all the worries out. I drop them, *plunk*, inside.

Mrs. Lullaby looks in my eyes and smiles. "Thank you, Sunny."

When Mrs. Lullaby sees me, I feel so happy-warm inside.

After she finishes collecting everybody's worries, Mrs. Lullaby opens up the window — *whoosh,* a blast of cold air and flurries fly in — and she throws the suitcase out.

"There," Mrs. Lullaby says, closing the window and smack-swipe-smacking her hands together. "Now we're free to learn."

The first time Mrs. Lullaby threw her suitcase out the window, we all gasped. Was our teacher fruit-loopy or what? "It's okay," Mrs. Lullaby said. "The worries are gone, but my suitcase will be back."

I pictured Mrs. Lullaby's beautiful silver suitcase outside on the dirty ground. What if somebody stole it? Then she wouldn't have it for her roller-coaster trips.

After school that day, I saw Mr. Birch, the so-nice-smiley janitor, hand the silver suitcase back to Mrs. Lullaby. "Thank you, Aaron," she said.

"Glad to help, Lucretia. Same time tomorrow, right?"

Mrs. Lullaby smiled. "Yes, that's right."

❀　❀　❀

In English, Mrs. Lullaby gives us an assignment to write a story about something fun we did over the holiday break. *Oh, good, I love to write.* Mrs. Lullaby says my words "move like music." Mrs. Lullaby copies her favorite lines from our work, "especially fine examples of beautiful writing," onto sheets of colored paper and hangs them on a clothesline that stretches across our classroom. I've got the most sheets of anybody. I know because I counted.

"You may read your stories at Morning Share Time on Friday," Mrs. Lullaby says. "As always, your parents are welcome."

Packing up at the end of the day, I hear Davina Bishop and Crystal Lord, two of the meanest bus-girls, talking. They went to Disneyland over vacation. Jazzy and I call them the bus-girls because they ride the yellow bus to school. They live in the pretty new houses up on Hill Street. I'll be taking that yellow bus some-day, too — when we buy our yellow house. Momma says any color house will do, but Daddy says, "If Sunny wants yellow, then yellow it will be."

Walking home, I'm excited to start writing my story. Jazzy and I stop at Mrs. Milo's. The little cupcake packages are on sale. I choose chocolate with vanilla frosting. Jazzy gets vanilla with chocolate frosting. There's a basket of mini candy canes marked *Free* on the counter. "Take some, girls," Mrs. Milo says, smiling.

That makes me think of my holiday. Maybe there's free candy everywhere you go! No wait, that's basically Halloween. Better than breakfast in bed, but still not good enough.

We take off our mittens and eat our cupcakes as we walk.

"So what's the new holiday going to be?" Jazzy says.

"I'm still working on it," I say. "Do you have any ideas, besides the Jell-O jigglers, I mean?"

"No, Sunny. It was your plan. I'm just going to help."

"I'll think about it tomorrow," I say.

First there was Girls' Night, then Visiting Day, then school, and right now my mind is sparkling with ideas for my story. It's going to be my best one ever.

"I hope Momma can come to Morning Share Time," I say to Jazzy.

Just once I hope she can come.

CHAPTER SEVEN

How Sunny Got Her Name

❀ ❀ ❀

The stars got jealous and
complained to God.

It's almost dark when Jazzy and I get home
from school with frozen noses. January sure is
Eskimo cold. Whatever new holiday I make
up will have to be sunny warm and bright as
the Fourth of July. But first I have to do my
homework.

Out in front of Riverview Towers, Jazzy and I
stop to make a snowkid. We made that name up

ourselves. One day we were wondering, how come people always make snowmen? What about snow-ladies and snowgrandmothers and snowkids?

You make a snowkid just like a snowman, except smaller. And they only take a few minutes to make. You just roll three fat snowballs and stack them up.

Mrs. Sherman will be looking at that ugly red-rooster clock in her kitchen, wondering where I am, so I hurry and roll the bottom ball. Jazzy does the middle. I stick the head on top. Jazzy pokes holes for eyes and a nose. I scoop out a smile. "There." Then I remember the candy canes. I pop them in like striped bunny ears. We stand back and look. Mrs. Gordon raps on her window, smiling and waving. She looks for us every day. Jazzy and I smile and wave back. "Hello, Mrs. Gordon!"

Inside the door, I stand on a crate and unlock

the mailbox marked *Holiday*. My daddy's name is Hercules. Momma is Sherry. They picked the name Sunny for me because Momma said the sun shined so bright and long the day I was born the stars got jealous and complained to God. "Sorry, stars," God said. "An especially sunny girl was born today."

Daddy says we share our last name with Miss Billie Holiday, one of America's most famous jazz singers. People say Momma sounds just like her. I love when Momma sings Miss Holiday's song "God Bless the Child." *Papa may have, Mama may have, but God bless the child that's got his own . . . that's got his own.*

I look through our mail. Bills, bills, junk. No letter from Daddy.

I buzz Mrs. Sherman in 4-B, and when she hears my name, she presses the button in her apartment and the front door unlocks. The lobby smells like food. Somebody's always cooking. Bacon, onions, fish, fries, garlic, curry, and spices I don't even know the names of. The smells soak into my hair and clothes. It's like living in a restaurant.

There are six kids at Mrs. Sherman's place today. I'm the only fourth grader. All the rest are little kids. I take off my boots and hang my coat inside the door.

"You're late, Sunny," Mrs. Sherman says, her smelly perfume almost knocking me out. She looks at the red rooster instead of me. "Wash your hands good, please, and have your snack."

"Yes, ma'am." I take two graham crackers and a cup of apple juice. That's the Monday menu at Mrs. Sherman's place. Tuesday is goldfish and grape juice. Wednesday is peanut-butter crackers and milk. Thursday is pretzels and orange drink.

Two kindergartners at the table laugh loudly about something.

"Shoosh! Be quiet," Mrs. Sherman says. "Mr. Sherman is resting."

I look at the door that's always closed. In all the times I've come here, I have never seen or heard Mr. Sherman, even once. I think Mrs. Sherman is making that man up. Either that or he's a ghost.

I take my snack and go into the "cave," my special spot behind the big, slouchy chair in the corner. I put my backpack at the entrance to keep intruders out. I've got so many sparkler ideas for my story, I can't wait to write them down. I peek out to make sure the coast is clear. No way am I going to sit at the table with the little kids, and I certainly don't like people standing over my shoulder judging my ideas when I'm still trying to figure them out myself. Especially people like

Mrs. Sherman. All she sees are mistakes. She never sees anything beautiful.

"That's spelled wrong." "That doesn't make sense." "Capitalize that." "Put a comma there. . . ." I tell you, that lady's a butterfly squisher.

Mrs. Sherman is busy bothering Louis Loomie right now. She's the hardest on him. I've got some time. I print my title:

Aloha, Hawaii
by Sunny Holiday

It was a sparkly blue day when our plane took off for Hawaii. I got the window seat. Momma and Daddy said it would take a whole day to get there, but I didn't care. We buckled up and then we were off! Up, up, up.

Down below on Earth, the cars looked like bees bumble-buzzing along the road. And then, a cloud sailed right by my window! It looked like cotton candy, good enough to eat, but you can't just open an airplane window and grab a cloud in out of the sky. . . .

Mrs. Sherman is heading my way. I hide "Aloha, Hawaii" and pull out my math sheet. I do a division problem quickly. Mrs. Lullaby says I'm an "absolute math marvel."

"Sunny," Mrs. Sherman says. "Stand up and show me your work, please."

I hand Mrs. Sherman my math sheet. She takes it without looking at my eyes. I don't know why she doesn't like me.

"You've only done one," Mrs. Sherman says, checking the rooster clock. She squinches her nose to show she's not happy, her nostrils big and round like the horse the police officer let Jazzy and me pet last summer. Boy, was that horse-doo stinky.

Mrs. Sherman huffs and hands me back the sheet. "Get busy, Sunny, please. I want all of your homework finished by the time your mother comes. That poor woman works hard all day. She doesn't have time to be helping you tonight."

"Yes, Mrs. Sherman," I say, smiling inside my head. Mrs. Sherman doesn't know my momma. No matter how tired Momma is, she'll want to hear all about my day, every bit, and what Jazzy and I saw on the way home, and she'll check all my homework and my take-home folder, and since Daddy's not here, Momma and I will make up a story, too. Momma will have time for all of that. And dinner, and dishes, and then her own homework.

Momma's college degree is going to take a very long time because she can only do one class a semester. She's going to be a nurse or maybe a doctor. Momma says college is the way to get a good job and a good life. I'm going to college for sure. Jazzy and I already decided. We're going to Harvard and we're going to be roommates and we're bringing Jade and Penny along.

Mrs. Sherman moves on to bothering Su-Gene about her spelling, poor kid, and I haul "Hawaii" back out. I've got the whole story spark-spark-sparkling in my head. I can hardly write fast enough. One line is so good it cracks me up, but I suck the giggles back in quick so Mrs. Sherman doesn't come snooping again.

I can't wait to see Momma's face when I read my story on Friday!

CHAPTER EIGHT

The Three-Thing Story

✿ ✿ ✿

Momma likes surprising me
with trash-treasures.

Momma comes to get me right when the rooster crows six, just like she promised. She looks so tired, but she doesn't complain. Under her coat, I can see Momma's wearing her uniform with her name tag, *Sherry,* and the *It's Another Great Day at the Crowne* button. Momma has to wear the same ugly gray uniform like all the workers. She can't sew on flowers or sparkles to make it a "Sherry Chic" original.

Even so, I bet my Momma stands out. She's the prettiest lady I know.

"I've got a trash-treasure for you," Momma says as we walk downstairs. She hands me a little red plastic heart about the size of a quarter. Her hands are rough from cleaning. "It was a decoration on a box of candy someone threw away."

Momma likes surprising me with trash-treasures from work. You can't take money or clothes or jewelry or any other personal items left behind in the rooms you clean. Only things clearly meant for the garbage.

"Thanks, Momma." I trace the heart in my hand. "It's beautiful."

Inside our apartment, Momma flicks on the light and turns up the heat. She puts the bills on the counter. "Let's get some comfy clothes on," she says.

Momma turns on the radio to the jazz station, 104.9 FM. She hums along as she makes our grilled cheese sandwiches and tomato soup. I clean Queen Jade's litter box, then I brush her and feed her and give her fresh water. I wash my hands and set the table. Momma pours our milk and lights the candles, just like in a restaurant.

We always have candles and flowers on our dinner table. Fresh flowers only. If there's one thing Momma and I cannot tolerate, it's fake plastic flowers on our table.

I am our family's official flower picker. Wild flowers like dandelions and violets and daisies. Momma says you don't have to be rich to have fresh flowers on your table. She says the hundred-dollar roses people toss in the trash at the Crowne never smelled better than lilies of the valley growing free and wild in the month of May in the empty lot on the corner. The lot that was supposed to be our park.

Lilies of the valley are my momma's favorite flowers. Dandelions are mine. I don't tell Momma, but dandelions are better than lilies.

Of course, you can't pick dandelions, or any other flowers, when it's wintertime in Riverton. Good thing the red poinsettia Mrs. Gordon gave us for Christmas is still going strong.

I tell Momma about Morning Share Time coming up on Friday. "It's from 8:30 to 9:05 A.M., and you can bring in breakfast treats. Make your famous banana muffins, okay?"

"I will definitely make the muffins, and I'll try my hardest to be there, Sunny." Momma gets the calendar and marks it down. "I'll ask Mr. Feeney tomorrow."

"Tell Mr. Meany you have a doctor's appointment or something."

Momma looks at me and scrunches her eyebrows together. I look the other way.

We don't tell lies in our family, but I know Mr. Meany doesn't care "one stinking bit" about school stuff. He got cancer last year, though, and so if you mention a medical-related reason for being late, that old meanie sometimes has a softer heart.

"I mailed your pictures to Daddy," Momma says. "He will be so surprised." Daddy might be only three hours away by ship, but sometimes it takes a whole month for him to get our mail. I hope he gets my package quick and writes back soon.

After dinner I get out the washable markers and add more words to our wall book. "*Sunshine . . .*

Fireflies . . . New years . . . New days . . . People who see you . . . Teachers who love you . . . Cotton candy clouds . . . Snowkids . . . Trash-treasures . . . Wildflowers . . ." I use all different colored markers for the words and I curve the lines like a rainbow. Our wall keeps getting more and more beautiful. Just wait until Daddy sees!

I take a step back and look up at my creation. It is marvelous. Hey wait, maybe every kid could make a wall book of their own on Kid's Day? Everybody's rainbow would be different, special with their favorite things. No . . . I bet lots of Mommas wouldn't allow markers on the wall. Jazzy's mother, Jo-Jo, would — but those bus-girls? *Nuh-huh.* Crystal Lord cried like a baby when she got red paint on her shirt in kindergarten. "Get it off, get it off!" she shouted to our teacher. "My mother will kill me!" Jazzy and I just rolled our eyes and kept painting our masterpieces.

Momma checks my homework (I keep "Hawaii" for a surprise), and then I pack up for tomorrow. When I get my pajamas on, Momma comes to sit with me on my bed. I read her a chapter of my book. We read together every night. "Keep a book by your bed and read every night, and soon, my friend, you'll be booked for life." That's what the author lady who came to our school said. I raised my hand and took the pledge. So far I haven't missed a day.

When Daddy's here, he and I make up a three-thing story. Daddy invented it. He's so good with ideas like that. I guess because he's an artist. The three-thing story has to include three things you noticed that day. Something I saw on the way to school or a trash-treasure Momma brought home from the hotel. Daddy's the best at three-thing stories. I'm getting better. Momma just likes to listen.

My mind is still sparkling about my Hawaii story and I almost want to show it to Momma *right now*, but I don't want to spoil the surprise for Friday.

Momma yawns. "Ready, Sunny?"

"Yes." I close my eyes for a minute and I think about my day. "Okay," I say. "The three things are: a snowkid, a poinsettia, and a tiny plastic heart."

"Good," Momma says, smiling. She leans her head back on my pillow and closes her eyes. I prop Valentine under her arm and cover them with my quilt.

"Once upon a time," I say, "there was a snowkid who lived underneath a giant poinsettia plant. He was pretty happy for a snowkid. He had eyes and a nose and a smile for a mouth, but he was missing one important thing . . ."

"*Mmm, mmm,*" Momma says, snuggling in with Valentine. "I just love your stories, Sunny."

CHAPTER NINE

Writer's Block

❊ ❊ ❊

Hopefully those fireflies are on their way.

I wake up extra early and tiptoe to the kitchen real quiet. I make a cup of cocoa in the microwave, pushing the top button early so the *beep-beep-beep* won't wake up Momma.

Back in my room, I sit on my bed with the pillows propped up, sipping my cocoa and reading over my Hawaii story, smiling, smiling, smiling. It's so good! I add in a few more colorful details.

There. The End. It's perfect. Just wait until Momma hears me.

I stand in front of my mirror and practice reading "Hawaii" — loud and proud with passion — like Mrs. Lullaby taught us, making good eye contact with my audience, Queen Jade.

Jade is absolutely mesmerized. I bet if those little white paws could clap, she'd give me a standing ovation. I take her in my arms and hug her close. I feel her wet nose against my cheek. I pet her and she licks my fingers. "I wish you could come to Share Time, Jadie. Maybe someday I can bring you to school. Maybe someday when Mr. Otis takes a vacation."

Now, time for Kid's Day. I wrap my quilt around me and sit at my desk. I take out a fresh yellow tablet, sharpen my pencil, then start to write "Kid's Day," but no, wait, my new January holiday needs a better name than that. But what?

I wait and wait and wait, but no sparklers spark. I tap my pencil. I look around. I huff and puff. I doodle some flowers, stars, and smiley faces.

I have writer's block.

Mrs. Lullaby says never to worry about that. She says the best ideas come when we're not even trying, not even expecting them, like fireflies flitting by you on a summer's night. The trick is to be ready, and when an idea lights up inside your imagination, catch it fast and write it down quick, quick, quick as you can. Otherwise, it will fly away.

But I don't have time for fireflies today. January twentieth is almost here. I need a plan right now. Maybe if I start with a title, give it a good name first . . .

I write *Kid's Day*, then erase it. Kid's Day is sort of boring.

Mother's Day. Father's Day. How about

Daughter's and Son's Day? Or, Son's and Daughter's Day? No, some kids don't have parents. They're living with relatives or in foster homes. Then the holiday wouldn't be fair for them.

Mr. Otis says a "kid" is a baby goat and children should be called children.

Children's Day? No. That sounds formal and not very fun. Sort of like Mr. Otis.

It's got to be something fun. I know. Fun Day! Sunday, Monday, Tuesday, Wednesday, Thursday, Friday, Saturday, *Funday*.

But then my holiday would have to be once a week, every eight days, which actually wouldn't be bad at all. Oh, no, this is getting too confusing.

"Sunny," Momma calls in her sleepy morning voice. "Time to get up."

"Okay, Momma." I slip my yellow tablet into my drawer.

Hopefully those fireflies are on their way.

CHAPTER TEN

The Smartest Fourth Grade

❀   ❀   ❀

*Like New Year's Eve ginger ale when you
dump in the little red cherries.*

"Sunny!" Jazzy shouts when I meet her down front in the morning. "Guess what! The mayor's coming here!"

"Pipe down!" Mr. Petrofino, our "Soup," shouts. *Soup* is short for superintendent. Mr. Petrofino takes care of our building. If you saw him, you might think he was a lawyer or an important businessman. He always dresses in a suit and tie, with a triangle handkerchief in his lapel pocket. Mr. Petrofino is up on a ladder, fixing something. "Show some respect," Mr. Petrofino says to us with a scowl. "People are still sleeping."

"Sorry, Mr. Petrofino," we say. When we were little, Jazzy and I used to giggle about him being the "Soup." What kind of soup is he? Vegetable? Chicken noodle?

"Sister Queen read it in the paper, Sunny. Mayor Little is coming here Friday night. He's running for reelection and he's kicking off his campaign right here at Riverview Towers. Isn't that great, Sunny? Then you can tell him about the new holiday you're creating and he can make it official. This is your big chance!"

"Why's the mayor coming here?" I ask, squinting my eyes, suspicious. "That man's only ever been here once. The time he planted those droop-sorry trees when he promised us a park. He should see those trees now, all bent down dead from the snow."

"Oh, *pu-leeze*, *Louise*, who cares about trees?" Jazzy says, shaking her head. "You're making a new holiday, Sunny! But it can't be *real* unless the president or the mayor or somebody says so. This is your big break." Jazzy stops and stares in my eyes. "Okay, what's the problem?"

"I haven't made up the holiday yet!"

"So what," Jazzy says. "It's only Tuesday. You've got three whole days."

"I don't know, Jazzy."

"Sunny, stop it right there, girl. You're always saying you can do whatever you set your mind to . . ."

"Okay, okay. I'll think about it."

"Just make sure there's candy," Jazzy says.

❀ ❀ ❀

After Mrs. Lullaby collects our worries and throws the silver suitcase out the window, she turns and says, "I have exciting news for you, smarties! As you know, the state language-arts test we've been preparing for is scheduled for next week."

We all groan. I raise my hand. "How is that exciting, Mrs. Lullaby?"

"Good question, Sunny," Mrs. Lullaby says, looking toward the door and then lowering her voice. "I have a secret to share."

We all lean forward, ears open wide.

"Remember the big practice test I gave you just before vacation?"

We shake our heads yes.

"Well, I graded them last night and guess what? You scored amongst the smartest fourth graders in the entire state."

At first nobody makes a sound. Then it sinks

in, and excitement bubbles up like New Year's Eve ginger ale when you dump in the little red cherries.

"Oh, yeah!"

"Ahh-haaa!"

"That's what I'm talking about!"

Everybody's shouting out, our faces all shining proud.

"*Shhh*," Mrs. Lullaby says, smiling, looking toward the door again. "Let's keep it a secret for now, okay? We don't want to make the other fourth-grade classes feel bad, now do we?"

I think about it. I look at Jazzy. We shrug our shoulders and scrunch our noses like, "What harm would a little bragging do?"

"Let's make a promise," Mrs. Lullaby says, raising her hand like she's saying the Pledge. "That we will keep on working as hard as we can so that when we take the real test next week, Mrs. Lullaby's smarties will be smarty-pants super-stars! Is it a deal?"

"YES," we shout, raising our hands, too.

The smartest fourth grade in the entire state. Wow!

Social Studies is next. When we open our books, something at the window catches my eye. A little black-and-white bird *peck-peck-pecking* against the glass like it's trying to get in. It flies off, then comes back and crashes against the pane. I run to the window and look down. The glass is cold against my nose. The bird isn't moving. I put my palms on the glass. Mrs. Lullaby is behind me. She puts her hand on my shoulder. "It's okay, Sunny. I bet it's just stunned. Probably got the wind knocked out of it. I'll ask Mr. Birch to check."

Back in my seat, I try to pay attention, but I'm thinking about the bird and about that glass wall between me and Daddy on Visiting Day. I always put my palm against the glass on my side, and he puts his palm up to match on his side. I can see him smiling and I can hear his voice, but all I can feel is cold, hard glass.

After lunch, Mr. Otis comes to our class to remind us about the state test. "I can't stress enough how important this test is," Mr. Otis says, peering out over his glasses like he's studying a spot on the wall at the back of our room. "This is serious, ladies and gentlemen. Everyone must do his or her absolute best. Absolute best. The future of New Hope Charter School depends on . . ."

I look at Mrs. Lullaby and she winks at me. I look at Jazzy and our eyes giggle. That never-smile principal is wasting his time. He's talking to the wrong baby goats. He doesn't know how smart we are. He doesn't know we're the smartest fourth grade in the entire state. Boy, won't he be surprised. Maybe he'll even smile!

CHAPTER ELEVEN

Sunny Invents a Holiday

❀   ❀   ❀

*And then tons of sparklers
are sparkling like crazy.*

At dinner, I tell Momma all about how I want to make a holiday. Her eyebrows rise up. She tilts her head and smiles. "That sounds like an interesting idea," she says.

"Jazzy and I were thinking about how there's no fun day for kids in January. It's so dead in Riverton. December has Santa Claus, but then it's fifty whole days until Valentine's in February. We think there should be a fun holiday for kids *every* month."

Momma laughs and spoons out a ladle of chili. The steam swirls up to her smile.

"What's so funny?" I ask, annoyed.

"I'm not laughing at you, Sunny. I'm just remembering how when I was little I said to my momma, 'How come there's a Mother's Day and a Father's Day, but no *Kid's Day*?'"

"Exactly! That's what I told Jazzy. And what did Grand-Gran say?"

"She said, 'Every day is Kid's Day.'"

"What's that mean?"

Momma laughs. "That's what I said. Grand-Gran meant that on Mother's Day and Father's Day children do something special for their parents to show how much they love them, but that parents do that for their children every day of the year."

I think about Jazzy's father not even remembering her birthday. "Not all parents," I say.

"You're right, Sunny."

"And it's not true that kids only do nice things for their parents on Mother's Day and Father's Day. I do nice things for you and Daddy all the time."

"You sure do," Momma says, nodding very seriously. "You make every day Mother's Day for me. That's the truth."

"So then it's not fair, right? If there's a Mother's Day and a Father's Day, there should be a Kid's Day, too."

"Seems logical to me," Momma says. "I think you're onto something, Sunny. And it sounds like fun. Speaking of which, we need to plan for Saturday. It's our turn to host Girls' Night. My travel agent must be on a cruise or something. That man hasn't returned any of my calls. I'm going to speak to his boss." She winks. "Where should we go?"

I caught a few fireflies on the way home, and my brain is starting to spark with ideas for Kid's Day right now. I don't want to get creative overload and explode. "I'll think about it tonight, okay?"

"Sure," Momma says. "I was thinking Italy or maybe Paris. Oh, and I have some news."

"Daddy?"

"No," Momma says. "It's about work. I heard Mr. Me-*Feeney* mention a certain celebrity who'll be staying in the Royal Suite this weekend. Somebody you like." Momma's eyes are twinkling like she's got a big secret.

"Who?"

"Guess."

"I don't know. Who? Tell me!"

"Somebody . . . . *sweet*," Momma says. "That's the clue, sweet."

Sweet, sweet . . . . . candy . . . .

"CANDY WRAPPER?!!"

"Yes," Momma says, laughing.

"No! Candy Wrapper is staying at your hotel!!? Oh, Momma, you have to get her autograph for me. Please, please!"

Momma laughs. "You know the rules, Sunny. No autographs."

"But, Momma . . ."

"Let's not think about that now. Right now, you need to do your homework."

I go to my room and start my spelling. *Candy Wrapper.* I just love her! She's mine and Jazzy's favorite girl rapper. Her last name is a homonym. Wrapper. Rapper. When kids go to her shows, they hold up their favorite candy wrappers and wave them in the air, "Can-*Dee*, Can-*Dee*!" I've seen them on television.

I would give anything if Jazzy and I could go to her concert. I'd be waving a yellow Mallo Cups wrapper. Jazzy would be waving M&M'S. Wait until Jazzy hears!

After I finish the state-test practice pages (what a breeze — we're so smart!), I start thinking about Kid's Day. I write down *Kid's Day — January 20*. We don't need a fancier name than that. "Keep it simple," Mrs. Lullaby says.

What would a holiday named Kid's Day be like?

At first nothing comes, but then sparklers start sparking in my head and I write as fast as I can:

"Candy — there has to be candy. And No School and..." And then tons of sparklers are sparkling like crazy and I don't worry about complete sentences or punctuation or spelling or anything — I just get it all down as fast as the ideas come, "...you can dress up like Halloween and have a big feast like Thanksgiving and presents like on Christmas and candy like on Valentine's Day and money under your pillow like from the tooth fairy and a pot of gold like on St. Patrick's Day and more candy like on Easter and fireworks like on the Fourth of July and a brand-new pool and a park and an ice-cream truck and a carnival in the Kmart parking lot where you can play games and win prizes and ride the Ferris wheel and roller coaster, a real Wildcat roller coaster, and there's a guaranteed good present like on your birthday, and parents have to do what their kids say all day long, and you can have anything you want for dinner, and there's no bedtime, and your best friend gets to sleep over, and everybody's happy, and the river gets cleaned up, and your momma doesn't have to work so hard, and your daddy gets out of prison and doesn't mind living in Riverview Towers, and this time he stays for good . . ."

I stop. I start crying. I cry so hard all the sparklers sputter out in the rain.

How are you, Daddy? Do you miss me? I hope you like the pictures. . . .

I pick up Valentine and hug him tight. We go to my calendar and count the days until the next time I can see Daddy. I hope it's not snowing then. I hope the ship's in good shape. I hope Daddy's still being good. Only five more months and he'll be free.

"Momma!" I say, running to the table where she's doing her homework. "We have to hurry and finish writing our book so it can get printed and we can get rich and you won't have to clean rooms but can just go to college and we can buy our house on Hill Street so Daddy will be happy and stay for good and . . ."

"Sunny," Momma says, putting down her pen. She looks shocked. "Honey, come here." I walk to the table. "Sit down," she says. I sit next to her and she moves her chair closer and leans forward so her eyes and my eyes lock. She takes my face in her hands. "Sunny, honey, it is not your job to worry about those things. Your job is school and taking care of Queen Jade. It's mine and Daddy's job to take care of all the rest."

"But, Momma, if we finish our book quick —"

"Sunny, listen to me. And listen good. There's no shortcut to the big dreams in life, like a college degree or a house. It takes a long time to earn those things. It takes hard work and determination. Step-by-step, day by day, one foot in front of the other."

I sniff and shake my head like I think Momma's wrong.

"Sunny . . . this is important. Please hear me. Do you see all those sad brothers holding their

dreams on slips of paper, waiting in line to play
the numbers at Mrs. Milo's in the morning?
Scratching shiny dollar tickets, hoping to get rich
quick?"

I nod my head yes.

"That's all a big lie, Sunny. Do you hear me? A
great big evil lie."

I stare into my momma's beautiful brown eyes.
I can see myself in there.

"You are a good, smart girl, Sunny Holiday.
And if you keep working hard and doing your
best at school, you will go to college someday, and
you'll find out what your gifts are, and you'll get
a job you are proud of . . ."

"But what about Daddy!" I shout. "If we don't
get out of Riverton soon, he's going to leave us for
good next time and then he'll never ever come
back!" A monster-scary sob slips out of my mouth,
and tears gush like a fire hydrant in August.

"Oh, honey." Momma takes me in her arms and hugs me so tight I think my skin will pop. "Sunny, my sweet girl. Please don't worry. I think your daddy learned his lesson this time."

She strokes my hair. I hear her whisper, "I sure hope he has."

❊   ❊   ❊

Back in my room, I look over my sparkler ideas for Kid's Day. I may have gone a little overboard. Like those letters to Santa with twenty wishes and you only get two of them. I narrow my ideas down to a few of the best things. I read it over and revise it again. Mrs. Lullaby says that's when fireworks happen, when you re-see your words.

Later, when I get up to go to the bathroom, I see Momma slumped over at the table. "Momma."

I shake her arm gently. She's asleep on American History.

Momma opens her eyes and yawns. "Thanks for waking me, honey. Oh, no. Look at the time. I've got to finish the Civil War tonight."

"Don't worry, Momma. You can do it. I'll make you a cup of tea."

CHAPTER TWELVE

Morning Share Time

❀ ❀ ❀

Bloom, bloom, bloom.

Momma can come to Morning Share Time! Whoopee, whoopee, whoopee! Mr. Meany's got a soft spot after all. Momma gets up early Friday and makes two dozen of her famous banana muffins with the cinnamon sugar butter melted on top. Just wait until those bus-girls taste them. Just wait 'til they see my momma. She'll be the prettiest mother there.

I put on my favorite yellow sweater and my jeans with the yellow-flower pockets. Momma's wearing her best purple dress and the earrings Daddy gave her that look like real diamonds. She's got her uniform in a bag so she can change when she gets to work.

"Big day for my girl," Momma says.

"Yep," I say. Morning Share Time this morning, then the mayor tonight.

We're putting on our coats when the phone rings.

My heart pounds. "Momma, please don't answer it. What if it's Mr. Meany?"

Momma picks up the phone. I watch her face.

"Hi, Dee-Dee," she says, raising her finger to me and smiling like, "Don't worry, this will only take a second." I keep watching her.

Momma stops smiling. She walks with the

phone into her bedroom and closes the door. I put my ear against it to listen.

"Dee-Dee, honey, calm yourself down. Don't worry about work. Get the baby and get out of there. Do you hear me? What? I know, I know. Do you have someplace safe to go? Good, go now. Don't worry about Feeney. I'll cover for you."

Momma comes out of her room, her face all sad. "Sunny, I'm sorry but . . ."

Anger spits out of my mouth. "No, Momma. You promised."

"Sunny, I'm sorry. One of the girls at work is having a serious problem . . ."

"I don't care about her. What about me?"

"Sunny." Momma walks toward me.

"Forget it, Momma, just forget it. I thought I could count on you." I rush out, pulling the door slam-shut behind me.

Momma follows. "Sunny, wait. Don't forget the muffins."

"I don't want your stupid muffins." I turn and run down the stairs.

❀　　❀　　❀

Jazzy can tell I'm not in the talking mood on the way to school. She's carrying the plastic container of banana muffins. Momma brought them to Jazzy and said, "Would you please bring these in for your class, honey? Otherwise they'll go to waste."

When Mrs. Lullaby collects our worries, I make believe I'm putting mine in the silver suitcase, but I'm still thinking about how mad I am at Momma. Why does she have to be so nice helping those ladies from work? What about me? *What about me?*

The bus-girl mothers come at eight even though Morning Share Time doesn't start until eight-thirty. They stand there in the doorway with their shiny pink mouths, holding matching pink boxes of donuts, probably the frosted kind with sprinkles on them, waving and winking and smiling at their daughters.

The meanest bus-girl of all, Davina Bishop, sits behind me. She's talking to her best friend, Crystal Lord. "Look, Crystal, check it out. She's wearing my jeans."

I lean back to listen.

"You sure?" Crystal says.

"Yeah, I'm sure. My mother gave them to the Salvation Army."

My stomach flip-flop-hops like a frog. They're talking about me.

Davina and Crystal giggle. "Nobody wears

jeans like that anymore," Davina says. "And look, look. She sewed *flowers* on them."

They laugh louder. My ears are on fire.

Then I hear Jazzy.

"*Shut up*," Jazzy shouts. "You're a liar, Davina Bishop. Sunny's not wearing your stinking old jeans. Who would want your nasty old . . ."

"Girls, girls," Mrs. Lullaby says, coming toward us.

I tilt my head up to the ceiling so the tears will slip back in. No way am I going to let those busgirls see me cry. I pick up a pen and draw a star on my jeans. Up, down, up, over, down. Then another and another. Up, down, up, over, down. Up, down, up, over, down, digging in so hard I can feel it on my skin.

"Let's welcome our guests, class," Mrs. Lullaby

says at eight-thirty, motioning to the parents to come in.

"Mommy," Davina shouts, running like a kindergartner to give her mother a hug. "Sit here, next to me."

Mrs. Lullaby calls on Davina Bishop to read her story first.

Davina struts up to the front of the room like her story won first place in a contest or something.

She's only going first because of alphabetical order. I look toward the door again and then out the window.

The bus-girl mothers have video cameras. They tape their daughters and clap loud afterward with tears in their eyes like it's the Academy Awards.

Jazzy looks at me and our eyes talk. Her mother isn't here, either.

"Jazzy Fine," Mrs. Lullaby calls next. Davina giggles behind me. I turn and look at her so hard I swear my eyes make sunburns on her stone-cold face.

Other kids read, and then Mrs. Lullaby says, "Sunny Holiday, it's your turn."

I look at Mrs. Lullaby and she nods, smiling so happy like she could barely sleep last night because she was so excited to hear my story, especially.

I walk slowly to the front of the classroom, hunched like one of Mayor Little's trees. I don't look at my audience the way Mrs. Lullaby taught us. I don't smile. I don't read in a loud proud voice.

I mumble my story like it's a definition from that dead old dictionary over there.

When I say "hula-dancing," I hear the giggles. When I get to the best part about the luau roast, I see Davina and Crystal clamp their hands over their mouths, but I can hear them snorting like *oinky-oink* pigs.

When I say, "The End," everybody claps nice, especially Mrs. Lullaby.

"Lovely, Sunny, just lovely," she says.

As soon as I sit back down, Davina leans forward and whispers, "Liar. You liar. River rats don't go to Hawaii and swim in the ocean. River rats swim in the river. The dirty old muddy river."

After the stories are finished, the bus-girls walk around the classroom passing out the sprinkle donuts from the matching pink boxes. The bus-girl mothers pour the juice.

"*Mmm, mmm*, these banana muffins are scrumptious, Sunny," Mrs. Lullaby says loudly so everyone can hear. "Your mother is a wonderful baker. Please tell her how much we appreciate her generosity."

I don't eat any pink donuts or muffins, either. I draw more black stars on my jeans. Up, down, up, over, down. Up, down, up, over, down. Up, down, up, over, down. So hard I nearly rip through the cloth.

At the end of the day, Davina and Crystal brush past me singing, "Hoo-laa-Hoo-laa-Hoo-LAA . . ."

I hear them singing in my head all the way home.

I'm never going to Girls' Night ever again. Stupid make-believe lie.

☘   ☘   ☘

I don't tell Momma what happened.

After dinner, the doorbell rings. It's Jo-Jo. She and Momma talk out in the hall. Momma comes into my room.

"Sunny," she says. "I'm so sorry about today. Jo-Jo told me what happened. Those little brats, treating another person that way. If I was their mother, I'd take a cake of soap to their nasty little mouths, so much soap they'd blow bubbles next time they talked."

I laugh and then *whooshhhhhh* . . . tears flow like a waterfall.

Momma rocks me strong in her arms. "There, there, baby. It's okay." She rubs my back. She strokes my hair.

"Always remember who you are, Sunny Holiday. The stars were so jealous the day you were born, they all went complaining to God."

I smile. Momma smiles more.

"And what's that your daddy always says about dandelions?"

I sniff. I shake my head.

"Come on, Sunny," Momma says. "I know you remember."

"A dandelion is a powerful flower. There's a lion in its name."

"That's right," Momma says. "That's right. *Grrrrrr, rrrrrr, rrrrr. ROAR!*"

I laugh and wipe my nose.

"You keep blooming like a dandelion, Sunny. And don't let anything or anyone keep you down. Do you hear me, girl? Bloom, bloom, bloom."

She hands me a tissue. I blow my nose and kiss her. "I love you, Momma. I love you so much. I'm sorry I was disrespectful this morning. I know you wanted to come."

"Don't worry about it, honey," Momma says. "That's history. And now the mayor's coming. Don't you have something to say to him?"

CHAPTER THIRTEEN

Vote Little for Big Changes

❀   ❀   ❀

Kids are just as important as grown-ups,
and we should have a holiday.

My plan is ready. I'm good to go. Just wait until the mayor hears me!

It's six-forty-five and Momma and me, and Jazzy, Jo-Jo, and Sister Queen, are dressed up Sunday-fancy to meet the mayor. We sit on the cold metal folding chairs in the front row of the Community Room, right up in front by the podium. Mr. Petrofino, the Soup, looks at us and nods. He

fixes his tie and handkerchief that don't need fixing and sets his eyes on the podium. Momma and
Jo-Jo's friends from Girls' Night are here. Mrs.
Gordon and Mrs. Hartman. Mrs. Gordon is wearing a mink coat. It is chilly in here.

Chief Slade, he's a firefighter who lives on the
sixth floor, asks Jo-Jo if the heat is working okay
in her apartment now.

She smiles, all happy talking to him. He winks
at Jo-Jo when he leaves, and Jazzy and I giggle.

Sister Queen nudges Jo-Jo hard with her elbow,
shaking her head and waving her hand back and
forth like she's fanning herself. "*Mmm-mmm*,
sure is hot in here."

"Momma, *shhhhh*," Jo-Jo says, laughing.

"Just reporting what I see, girl," Sister Queen
says. "That brother's got his eyes on you."

"Momma, stop," Jo-Jo says, looking at me and
Jazzy. "Little ears are listening."

Jazzy and I giggle harder. We know the chief likes Jo-Jo. The whole building does. We've got a bet going when he's going to ask her out. Jazzy bet February. I bet March. I think Jazzy's going to win.

Mrs. Sherman sits down behind us, smelly perfume coating the room like disinfectant spray. No Mr. Sherman in sight. I tell you, she is making that man up.

Miss Fontenot tap-dances into the room, wearing a shimmery, silvery dress that jingles as she moves. She swerve-sways to the front of the room and looks around spooked — like, "What are you all doing here?" Then she sits in the corner and folds her hands on her lap.

Jazzy and I keep looking to see if she's going to dance again, but she doesn't.

I'm holding copies of my Kid's Day plan, all

printed on sunny yellow paper. Mr. Feeney let Momma use the copy machine at work. I swear something is melting inside of him.

Boy, is Mayor Little going to be surprised! But he'll have to get moving quick-quick-quick if he's going to make Kid's Day official for January twentieth.

The door keeps opening with reporters coming in, putting microphones up on the podium. I counted, and all of the TV stations are here: 6, 9, 10, 13, and 23.

"There's Liz Bistle from Channel Six," Jo-Jo says. "She's great."

"And that's Elaine Dallas from Channel Thirteen," Momma says. "Isn't she pretty?"

A skinny lady in a gray suit and blond hair is rushing around the room telling people to do this and that. She sees me and Jazzy. She stares at us.

She opens her briefcase, takes out a folder, and checks something. She walks over to us. "You're the girls from the tree-planting ceremony, right?"

"Yes," Jazzy and I say, like sister-twins.

"Perfect," she says. "Stay right here in the front row." She hands us each a shiny strip of paper that says, *Vote LITTLE for BIG Changes*.

"What's this?" I say.

A man with a badge that says *Times Union Newspaper* is listening to us.

"It's a bumper sticker for your car," the blond lady says, smiling.

"We don't have a car," I say. "Neither does Jazzy."

The man with the *Times Union* badge laughs and writes something down. The blond lady's red mouth is smiling at me, but her blue eyes look mad. "Then put it on your school book bag," she says, sugar-sweetly. She turns and walks to the podium. "Good evening, ladies and gentlemen, thank you for coming . . ."

I wonder why she doesn't thank us kids for coming, but I'm not complaining. I know what I'm here for.

"I'm the mayor's press secretary, Ricky Kissane," the blond lady says. "It is a pleasure to be here with you tonight. I'm sure everyone has busy schedules this evening so, without further ado, please join me in a warm Riverview Towers welcome for our mayor . . . Riverton's very own native son . . . Mr. Rockefeller Little the Third."

We all clap.

"You look good," Jazzy whispers to me. I'm wearing my yellow sweater.

Mayor Little walks up to the podium and says, "Thank you, Ricky. Thank you very much." He fixes his tie. He looks at the clock on the wall. He sees me and Jazzy and waves at us like we're little kids. Ricky Kissane whispers something and the mayor looks at me and Jazzy again. "Oh, yes, of course." He motions to us. "Girls, please come up here and take a bow."

Jazzy and I do what he says. He asks us our names. Mayor Little puts an arm around each of us like we're buddies and turns us toward the cameras. "It's so good to see my two young friends, Jazzy and Sunny, again. These girls were with me the day we broke ground on phase one of the Riverton Beautification Initiative, just one of the many exciting projects I'm committed to . . ."

The mayor nudges Jazzy and me to go back to our seats. He talks on and on and on.

I am listening.

I'm waiting to hear him mention the playground.

I'm waiting to hear him mention the pool.

I'm waiting to hear him mention cleaning up our part of the river.

". . . and so that we may continue together revitalizing Riverton, building on the strong momentum of this first term, I come here tonight to humbly ask for your support as I formally announce my candidacy for a second term as mayor of the fine town of Riverton, New York."

There's some clapping, but not as loud as before.

"Thank you, thank you very much," Ricky Kissane says. "Now, Mayor Little would love to take questions, but he has another commitment this evening. Please feel free to call or write with your comments and suggestions, and the mayor will be glad to —"

Two men in suits are whisking Mayor Little away. Jazzy nudges me with her elbow so hard I yelp. "Go, Sunny. Now," she says. "Stand up and say something. This is your chance."

I run up quick to the microphone and pull it down. I clear my throat and say "Hello" in a loud proud voice like Mrs. Lullaby taught us. "Excuse me, Mayor Little, I have something to ask you."

The room gets quiet. The Channel 6 TV camera swings around to face me and then the others follow.

Mayor Little stops and turns around. The cameras turn to face him. My stomach is swishing like the basement washing machine on the heavy-duty cycle. The mayor looks at me, then at the TV cameras. He smiles a great big smile. "Why certainly, young lady. Snazzy, is it? I always have time for my constituents. What can I do for you?"

The TV cameras swing to face me. My heart is pounding. It's hot as Hawaii in here. All these lights on my face. All these people looking at me.

I might be on TV tonight. Maybe Daddy will be watching!

"Well, actually, Mr. Mayor, my name is Sunny, Sunny Holiday, and there are a few things you can do for me. Not just for me alone, but for all my neighbors here who voted for you."

A flutter of laughter floats across the room. My face is so flaming, you could roast marshmallows on it. Mayor Little looks mad. I look at Jazzy. She smiles. I look at Momma. She curls her hands up like paws and moves her mouth like a lion roaring. That almost makes me laugh.

I turn to the mayor. "Well, first, Mayor Little, with all due respect, you could turn that nasty lot on the corner into a park like you promised so that kids have a place to play."

Jazzy claps and shouts, "That's right!"

"And then, you could fix the broken pool so we can swim. August is horrible hot here."

"You tell it, girl," Sister Queen shouts, and people clap.

I gulp and keep on going. "And then, you could work on cleaning up our part of the river, that ugly fence, and the litterbug-covered rocks. It would be nice to stick our toes in that water. I realize a river is a very long thing, but we've been waiting a very long time."

People are clapping and cheering like crazy now. Was that a smile on Mr. Petrofino's face? The reporter from the *Times Union* shouts, "*Shhhh,* let her finish!"

My heart's beating so hard, I'm afraid it will burst. "And you could come visit New Hope Charter School to see how hard we're trying. You came for the party when we opened, but we haven't seen you since. And . . . I promised I wouldn't tell the secret, but guess what? My class, Mrs. Lucretia Lullaby's class, is the smartest fourth grade in the whole state!!"

I look at Jazzy and she's rocking back and forth with her hands in the air like, "Oh, ye — ah, oh ye — ah, that's my best girl, *are you hearing her*?"

"And, in conclusion . . ." I say, because I always like the sound of that when a grown-up is giving a speech, "you could proclaim January twentieth a new holiday in Riverton."

There's a ripple of noise around the room. Elaine Dallas from Channel 13 is asking Momma something. I'm feeling less nervous now.

"You could be the first mayor in the whole state, in the whole country, in the whole world, to say that kids are just as important as grown-ups and we should have a holiday. Think about it, Mr. Mayor. There's a Mother's Day and there's a

Father's Day. There should be a Kid's Day, too. I say it's time to vote Little for big changes!"

Jazzy jumps up and starts clapping and the whole room copies her. Everybody's clapping and whooping and cheering and high-fiving. Miss Fontenot tap-dances up to the front of the room and does a solo for everybody. Mr. Petrofino joins her.

Liz Bistle from Channel 6 sticks a microphone in the mayor's face. "And what do you say in response, Mayor Little?"

"I say I want this young lady on my team."

CHAPTER FOURTEEN

Stars Shining Bright

✿   ✿   ✿

I just want us to be together, that's all.

And that's how I got to be Junior Deputy Mayor of Riverton, New York. Momma says someday I'll be president.

The newspapers are calling me "the holiday girl."

My office is right here in the corner of the Community Room at Riverview Towers. My office hours are Saturday mornings from ten to eleven, but I'll stay as late as my constituents need me.

Once a month, Mayor Little sends his limousine to pick up me and Jazzy. The mayor's chauffeur, Mr. Namesh, is such a nice man.

The mayor and Jazzy and I do lunch at Jack's Oyster House. We sit in the big, red leather, cushy corner booth way in the back, the one reserved for the mayor.

I tell Mayor Little what people are concerned about, especially the kids, and he listens and takes notes. Jazzy and I order whatever we want from the menu: appetizer, salad, main course, dessert, and refills of ginger ale with cherries. We take home kitty bags for Jadie and Penny.

At our first meeting, the mayor and I agreed that we didn't have enough time to plan Kid's Day for this January, so I am "constituting a committee" that will work "under my direction" all this year to put the plans in place so that next January twentieth will be the first official Kid's Day in Riverton, New York!

Jazzy said, "No way are the bus-girls going to be on the committee."

I said, "Well, maybe they can bring the donuts."

Mayor Little said the "action plan" will be to first make Kid's Day a state holiday and then a national holiday. "Why not the whole world?" I said.

Mayor Little laughed and said, "That's the ticket. Thinking Big. I like your style, Sunny Holiday."

❀   ❀   ❀

I must be honest and confess that when I gave my speech in the Community Room that night, I was just planning on asking the mayor about making a Kid's Day holiday. But when I saw my neighbors and opened my mouth, all those other thoughts flew out like fireflies.

"High time somebody spoke up," Sister Queen said.

After I finished talking to all the reporters, Momma and me and Jazzy and Jo-Jo went to Mrs. Milo's for hot chocolate. Then we stopped at Daisy's Lucky Buck so Jazzy and I could spend the five dollars each that Sister Queen gave us!! I bought a journal and a sparkle pen and a Valentine's necklace for Momma — that's the next holiday — and matching sister-twin bracelets for me and Jazzy. Then we hurried home to watch the news.

There I was, on TV! Not just one, but all the channels.

Momma kept switching from 6 to 9 to 10 to 13 to 23, and there I was, and Jazzy, and Momma and Jo-Jo, and even Miss Fontenot dancing.

Queen Jade purred, and I said, "Don't worry, Jadie. I'll bring you next time."

We had popcorn and toasted with ginger ale and cherries like it was New Year's Eve. I couldn't wait to write on our wall book. And then the telephone rang.

Momma answered and turned away with her finger in her ear so she could hear. Oh, no, not Mr. Feeney.

Momma turned back around and handed me the receiver. "It's for you, Sunny."

"Hi, baby," Daddy said. My eyes filled with happy tears.

"I saw you on TV. I told everybody to quiet down. 'That's my girl!' I said."

It sounded like Daddy was crying, too. "I'm proud of you, Sunny." Long pause. "I'm sorry." *Sniff,* long pause. "I won't ever let you down again, honey, I promise. I'm so sorry!"

"It's okay, Daddy." I paused and took a deep breath, not letting him off the hook too quick. "Just keep being good, okay?"

Daddy laughed. "I will, baby. I promise. I can't wait to come home. I can't wait to see that wall book you're making. Momma says it's beautiful. And by June when I get out, your new park should be finished and the pool opened, too, and maybe I can teach you how to fish on the river like I used to when I was a kid."

"I'd like that, Daddy. And guess what? I was thinking about your big break. You've got to take your art portfolio out and show it to people, Daddy. Nobody's going to see it stuffed under the bed. And I've got connections now, you know.

Maybe the mayor can help you get a good job. You know, just until your big break comes."

"Thank you, baby," Daddy said. "But don't you worry about me. I'm going to take better care of you and your momma. I promise."

"Just keep loving us, Daddy. And stay. Just stay. I don't care about a house. I care about our family. I just want us to be together, that's all."

❀ ❀ ❀

The next day was Saturday. It was me and Momma's turn to host Girls' Night, but with all the excitement we hadn't even started planning.

When I came into the kitchen for breakfast, Momma was talking on the phone. "Okay, thanks so much," she said. "I've got to go."

"Who was that?" I said.

"Just someone from work."

"You don't have to go in today, do you?"

"No," Momma said, looking mysterious.

"Good. Then what should we do for Girls'
Night tonight?"

"Sunny, listen. Let me take care of it this time.
Okay? You've had a big week and I know you
want to study for that important state test."

"Are you sure you don't want any help?"

"No, baby. I've got it covered."

Later that morning, Jazzy called and said
Jo-Jo was treating us to an "afternoon of beauty"
at Crowns of Glory for doing such a good job
on TV.

We got our nails and our toes polished. When
Jo-Jo braided my hair, she put in some shiny
stars. "You're a celebrity now, Sunny," she said.
We even got makeup.

After, we went back to Jazzy's apartment and snuggled up on the couch to watch a movie with Sister Queen. I fell asleep.

The next thing I knew, Sister Queen was shaking my arm and saying, "Time for Girls' Night, Sunny."

Jo-Jo handed me a black cape from the beauty salon to wear. This one was painted all special with sparkly silver stars.

"Jazzy made it for you," Jo-Jo said.

When we got to my door, I heard voices and laughing inside. Jo-Jo rang the buzzer. It got quiet. Someone opened the door. The lights were off. It was dark inside. "You go in first, honey," Jo-Jo said to me.

I walked in.

"SURPRISE!!!!!"

Momma planned a Girls' Night party in

Hollywood, California, special just for her "little star." Me!

And guess what? Mrs. Lullaby came! And Mrs. Milo and Daisy from Lucky Buck's and even Miss Fontenot, who has never, ever come to a party before.

"I'm going to need my toes to pray thank you tonight," I said.

Momma's eyes filled with happy tears. "Me, too, baby. Me, too."

The phone rang.

It was Grand-Gran saying congratulations. "I want your autograph," she said.

And then, if that wasn't the hands-down-double-Dutch-backward-flip-and-back-again very best night ever in my *whole entire life*, the phone rang again.

You're never going to guess.

Candy Wrapper!!!!!!!!

"No way, no way." I kept shaking my head.

Jazzy was screaming in my ears.

"Come here, Sunny," Momma said, motioning me to come to the phone. "Come on, honey, hurry up, come here."

My feet were stuck frozen in the floor.

So Momma put Candy Wrapper on speaker phone, and Candy Wrapper sang a song right from her suite at the Crowne Plaza hotel dedicated to "Miss Sunny Holiday."

I couldn't speak, but finally I managed, "Jazzy, are we in heaven?"

❀   ❀   ❀

After everyone went home from Hollywood, Momma and I took the stairs up to the beach. We stood there, arm in arm, looking up at the sky.

"Same moon shining on Daddy tonight," I said.

"Same stars shining, too," Momma said. "And wait . . . listen. Do you hear them?"

"Who?"

"The stars. Don't you hear them? They're complaining again. 'Sunny Holiday . . . you stop right now. You're making us look bad, girl. Shining so bright like you are.'"

Momma and I laughed and my heart was so happy, I could feel it blooming like a dandelion.

Acknowledgments

✿   ✿   ✿

With my sincerest thanks to . . .

The girls of my hometown, Troy, New York, especially the students at School 14. I hope you'll keep writing in journals. Pour out your hearts and plant your seeds. If you can dream it, you can do it.

Tracey and Josh Adams, my agents, for loving Sunny from the start.

My editors, David Levithan, for letting Sunny be real, and Jennifer Rees, for wise and wonderful advice, and to everyone at Scholastic Press for bringing their talents to this project.

ACKNOWLEDGMENTS

My friend forever in spirit, Micki Nevett, outstanding champion of children's literature and book sparkler extraordinaire, who first heard Sunny's voice at the BFS restaurant in Albany and said, "Oh, Coleen, I've got goose bumps."

My friend Debbie Dermady, masterful teacher, unwavering cheerleader, in celebration of all of the young readers you inspire.

My friend Jennifer Groff, who challenged me to "find Sunny's truth."

My friend Donna Ginn, who says "stories are given to us for a reason."

My brilliant brother Jerry Murtagh and trusted friends Laurie Halse Anderson, Kim Soyka, Rachel King, Carol Chittenden, and Grace Bennett, for fanning on the first tiny sparks of Sunny.

My friend and author Debbi Michiko Florence, for the generous and joyful light you shine on all of us in the children's lit community.

My friend Frank Hodge, for our wonderful chats at Hodge Podge Books. Thanks for "collecting" me, Frank.

My friends and writing partners: Ellen Laird, Robyn Ryan, Eric Luper, Nancy Castaldo, Rose Kent, Karen Beil, Heather Norman, Lois Feister Huey, Kyra Teis, Liza Frenette, and Helen Mesick for nurturing the best in me.

My dear Ya-Yas and charter members of the "dance parties," Kathy Johnson, Ellen Donovan, and Paula Davenport. Dance your pants off, girls.

My mother, Peg Spain Murtagh, who should be awarded honorary doctoral degrees in faith, hope, love, and kindness.

Posthumously, to my father, Gerald T. Murtagh, who got up and went to work every morning to support six children, maybe always dreaming of being an artist.

My son Connor, for Sunny's name.

ACKNOWLEDGMENTS

My son Chris, for the Kid's Day ideas.

My son Dylan, for always wanting to read my new stories.

I love you all so much.

And, to all kids, everywhere . . . fingers crossed for that holiday! ☺

— CMP

About the Author

Coleen Murtagh Paratore is the author of the acclaimed The Wedding Planner's Daughter series as well as *The Funeral Director's Son* and *Mack McGinn's Big Win* and several picture books. The mother of three teenage sons, she lives in upstate New York and on Cape Cod, Massachusetts. Visit Coleen online at www.coleenparatore.com.

A holiday just for kids?

COLEEN MURTAGH PARATORE

Sweet and Sunny

As the Junior Deputy Mayor of her town, Sunny has a
mission: to create a national holiday called Kid's Day!
It will take a little work, but if anyone can make this
special day shine, it's Sunny!

SCHOLASTIC

www.scholastic.com

SUNNY2